Benjamin Gardiner

Indian Club Swinging

By an amateur

Benjamin Gardiner

Indian Club Swinging
By an amateur

ISBN/EAN: 9783337304126

Printed in Europe, USA, Canada, Australia, Japan

Cover: Foto ©Andreas Hilbeck / pixelio.de

More available books at **www.hansebooks.com**

BY AN

AMATEUR.

―――――

"For want of EXERCISE, appetite fails; for want of EXER-CISE, comfortable bodily warmth is not sustained; for want of EXERCISE, refreshing sleep is not obtained."—Maclaren.

PROVIDENCE:

E. L. FREEMAN & CO., PRINTERS AND PUBLISHERS.

1884.

" Ah! what avail the largest gifts of Heaven,
    When drooping health and spirits go amiss?
How tasteless then whatever can be given!
    Health is the vital principle of bliss,
And exercise of health. In proof of this,
    Behold the wretch who slugs his life away,
Soon swallow'd in disease's sad abyss;
    While he whom toil has braced, or manly play,
Has light as air each limb, each thought as clear as day."

—THOMPSON.

INTRODUCTION.

EXERCISE, THE LAW OF OUR BEING.

Every well informed person is aware that wholesome and vigorous exercise is indispensable to the enjoyment and preservation of health. This is the physical law of our terrestrial life. Milton assumes that the same law prevails in the celestial sphere, when he pictures the young immortals engaged in active sports at the gate of Eden.

> "Betwixt these rocky pillars Gabriel sat,
> Chief of the angelic guards, awaiting night;
> About him *exercised heroic games*
> The unarmed youth of Heaven."

THE CHEAPEST AND MOST CONVENIENT KIND.

The exercise with the Indian Club, while excelled by none in prompt and beneficial results, is at once the least expensive and the most convenient of modern recreations. These qualities of cheapness and convenience strongly commend it to that large class in every community which lacks either the means or the leisure to indulge in more elaborate and costly diversions. The expense of the club-swinger's equipment, including a light and a heavy set of clubs, a suitable habit, and an instruction book, need not exceed the moderate sum of ten or fifteen dollars. Thus, as compared with riding, boating or by-

1*

cycling, the original outlay is trifling, while the subsequent incidental expenses are merely nominal. The use of the clubs also comports with the utmost economy of time. To improve the circulation of the blood and impart vitality to the system a half hour's exercise with the clubs is fully equivalent to two hours brisk walking, or three-quarters of an hour in the saddle or on the wheel. Again, the clubs are always at hand. The exercise may be enjoyed at whatever hour of the day or evening may be found most convenient and at whatever place; at home,* in the hall or veranda of your cottage, or in the humming workshop; in inclement weather as well as clear; alone, or with companions. Where else may the toiling student, the sedentary mechanic, and the busy accountant find an exercise, combining so pleasantly physical culture and recuperation with mental relaxation, at once so inexpensive, so accessible, and so chary of precious time?

ITS SALUTARY EFFECT.

Club-swinging promotes appetite and digestion by quickening the circulation of the blood, while, by dispelling nervous excitement, it invites continuous and refreshing sleep. More directly it tends to strengthen the

---

* A strong argument in favor of Indian Club swinging is based on its perfect adaptation to home exercise, precluding the necessity of daily visits to the rink or gymnasium,—often at inconvenient distance; often demanding night attendance; not unfrequently cramped for space, and deficient in ventilation; if not open to more serious objections in respect to the formation of youthful habits and associations. Every boy should be provided with light clubs and an instruction book, and encouraged to use them at home.

> " Stay, stay at home, my heart, and rest;
> Home-keeping hearts are happiest,
> For those that wander they know not where,
> Are full of trouble and full of care;
> To stay at home is best."

wrist and arms; to expand the chest, producing deeper respiration; to brace the shoulders, and to straighten and invigorate the spinal column, thereby inducing the habit of erect posture and graceful carriage.

POSITION.

The attitude appropriate to this exercise may be termed oratorical, such as Webster or Everett might assume, calmly surveying a popular assemblage. The figure should be perfectly erect, looking directly forward; shoulders well back, arms at the sides with the elbows held in; palms of the hands turned partially to the front; knees straight, and the toes turned well out; thus presenting the human form as a statue, motionless, dignified and placid.

GRASPING THE CLUB.

The most easy and natural way of grasping the club is also the most correct. The hand should be closed firmly close to the ball of the club, the thumb being extended along the handle in order to control its movements in sweeping the large circles and arcs. In the smaller circles and wrist movements, the head of the club must be released, the thumb and forefinger only clinging to the handle.

THE SUITABLE WEIGHT.

In the selection of clubs, due regard should be paid to the size and physical condition of the performer. Each one should test his ability by swinging clubs of different calibre to a horizontal position, either in front or at the side, at the height of the shoulders. A club which can be placed in this position and held a few seconds without fatigue is suitable for rudimentary practice. In most cases, a club weighing two and a half or three pounds is heavy enough for beginners. Invalids should commence with even lighter weights. When skill is acquired and the arms are rendered hard and strong by habitual exercise, heavier clubs may be assumed with safety. The ponderous clubs sometimes wielded by professional athletes are not recommended for ordinary use.

EXACT MOVEMENT.

Precision of movement is of the utmost importance in club-swinging, and should receive careful attention from the commencement of the study. A careless and slovenly manipulation is alike distasteful to the beholder and useless to the performer. Lay every motion to the line and plummet. Let the club be held precisely vertical, precisely horizontal or precisely to the angle of forty-five degrees. Sweep the circles with perfect poise and deliberation, conceding to each its largest diameter and a uniform and unvarying contour.

LENGTH OF SWEEP.

The circles traced with the clubs vary in dimension. The largest have a diameter equal to twice the length of the arm and club. The diameter of the smallest is twice the length of the club. The dorsal or back circles being traced with the bent arm, have a variable diameter, always longer than twice the length of the club, but less than twice the length of the arm and club. Figure 8, exhibits the relative size of these three classes of circles.

STARTING POINTS.

The various points of departure are taken with reference to the foot of the club, of which points the following five are the principal, viz. : The foot of the club, first as it hangs vertically downwards at the side ; second, as it is held perpendicularly above the head ; third, as it is held on either side at an angle of forty-five degrees above the horizontal line of the shoulders ; fourth, as it is held vertically upwards in front of the breast ; fifth, as it is held horizontally at arm's length in front, at the height of the shoulders. These points which are sufficiently definite for reference and description are numbered 1, 2, 3, 4, 5, and are plainly illustrated in the first five engraved diagrams. Other starting points will be adverted to as they occur in the text.

THE HABIT.

When taking exercise, the person should be lightly apparelled in order to allow absolutely free and unhampered motion to the limbs and body. For class drill, a loosely fitting habit of soft flannel, as shown in figure 6, is both convenient and becoming. The fashion of the uniform is not so material, as that it should be light and easy fitting, suitable regard being paid also to the strength and durability of the fabric.

DENOTATION.

The nomenclature consists in the assignment of specific letters to denote the various circles and arcs used in club-swinging. It greatly facilitates lucid description, furnishes a simple formula for each swing, obviates the necessity of complicated diagrams, and renders self-instruction practicable and comparatively easy in cases where the text-book is the only available source of information. The large circles are denoted by the letters A B C D E F G H I J ; the small circles by l m n o p q r s ; the medium circles by w x y z.

PREVALENCE OF THE EXERCISE.

In our own country the Indian club exercise is steadily gaining in popular appreciation, while beyond the sea it is justly held in high repute and recognized by all classes, from prince to peasant, as a valuable agent in restoring and preserving health. Poets, familiar with the customs and pastimes of the old world, frequently allude to this and other manly recreations, pursued even by royal personages as an indispensable part of their early physical education. Longfellow represents King Olaf as

" Trained for either camp or court,
Skilful in each manly sport,
   Young and beautiful and tall;
Art of warfare, craft of chaces,
Swimming, skating, snow-shoe races,
   Excellent alike in all."

CHAPTER I.

SECTION 1.

LARGE FRONT, SIDE AND HORIZONTAL CIRCLES: OBLONGS.

FOUR FRONT CIRCLES.

A.

Taking a club in each hand, assume naturally and without stiffness or constraint the swinger's attitude as heretofore described and as illustrated in the first engraving. It is well, also, in your early practice to toe a line on the floor, making the sweeps of the club with reference to that line, either in the same plane or in vertical planes parallel to it, or cutting it at right angles as the case may be, in order to foster and develop as quickly as possible the habit of precision.

From the first point of departure, which is the foot of the club as it hangs at the side, swing the left club to the right, describing, with straight arm, a complete circle in front of the person. Make this circle several times, repeating the letter by which it is denoted. In like manner swing the right club to the left five or six times, describing a similar straight-arm circle in front of the person, repeating each time either mentally or audibly as you may prefer, the significant letter A; the object in every case being to associate together the circle and the letter which designates it. The two circles now described, although swept in opposite directions, are properly denoted by the same letter as both are swept inwardly across the person of the swinger. The circle A as traced by the left and right club is shown by dotted lines and arrows in the first engraving. Now, sweep the circle with both clubs, each in turn tracing the outer curve, both clubs starting at the same moment.   Also sweep the circle, starting the left club half a revolution in advance of the right.

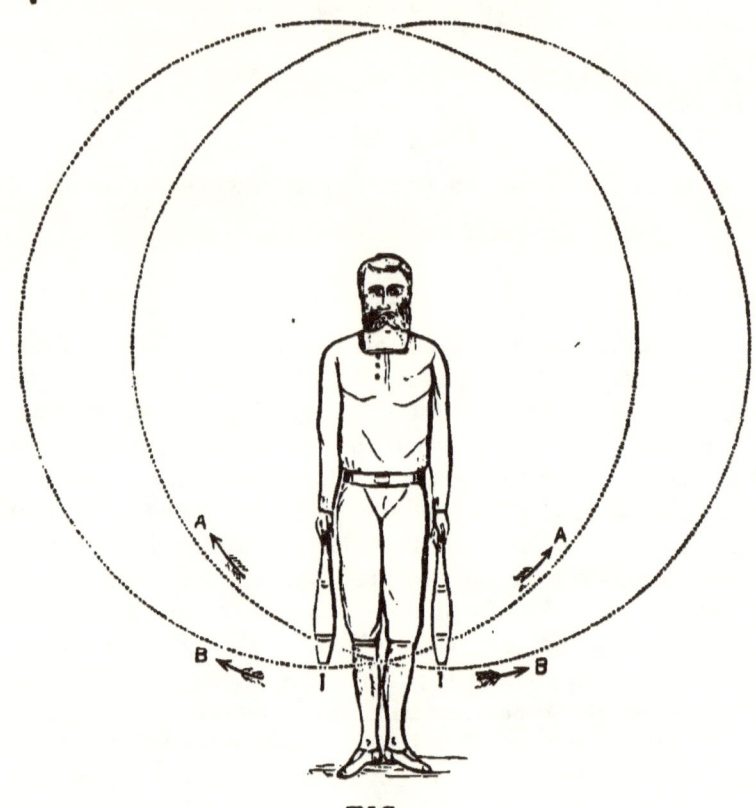

FIG. 1.

B.

From the same point swing the left club to the left, describing five or six times in succession a full-sized straight-arm front circle, associating with this movement the letter B.   Also swing the right club to the right, describing several times a similar circle and repeating its significant letter.   Both these circles being swept outwardly from the person of the performer, in the vertical plane of the floor line, are properly denoted by the same letter.   (See first engraving.)   Describe this circle also with both clubs, each in turn tracing the outer curve, both clubs leaving the goal at the same moment. Describe it also, starting one club half a revolution in advance of the other.

C.

Now reverse the position of the clubs by swinging them up, on the arc of the circle B to the second point of departure, where they are held perpendicularly at arm's length above the

Fig. 2.

head. From this point move the left club to the right making, five times, a full-orbed front circle, associating with this movement the letter C. Make a similar circle five times by moving the right club to the left, repeating the same significant letter.

2

These circles again are swept in opposite directions, but, never-theless, are properly denoted by the same letter, inasmuch as both of them are described by sweeping the club inwardly across the person of the swinger. The two circles denoted by C are shown in the second engraving. Describe this circle also with both clubs moving simultaneously, that is, starting at the same instant, then alternately, that is, one starting ahead of the other.

D.

From the same point **2,** pass the left club to the left, describing a complete straight-arm circle in front of the person, repeating the movement several times and designating it by the letter D. Describe similar circles by passing the right club to the right, associating the letter with the movement. These two classes of circles both move outwardly from the person, and ter-

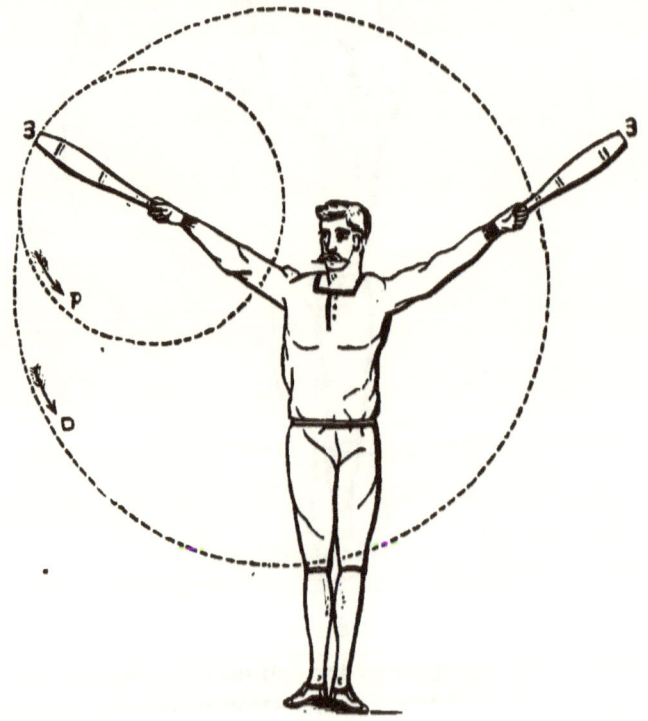

Fig. 3.

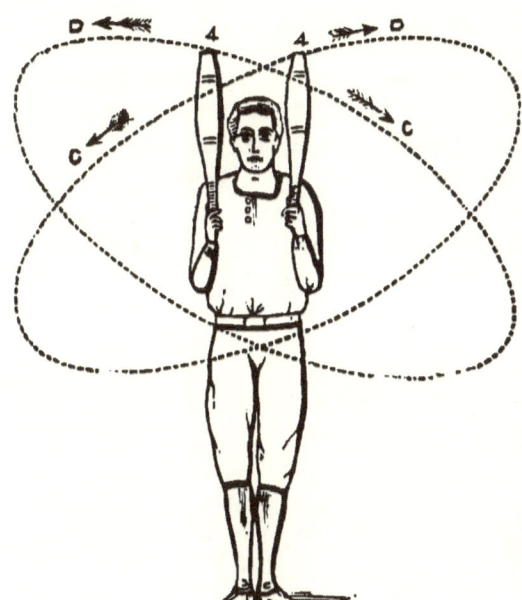

Fig. 4.

minate at the point of departure 2. They are shown in the second engraving. Return the clubs on the D arcs to the first position, which is a position of rest as well as a point of departure. (Other positions of rest are shown in the fourth, sixth and seventh engravings.) Describe D with both clubs, moving, first simultaneously, then alternately.

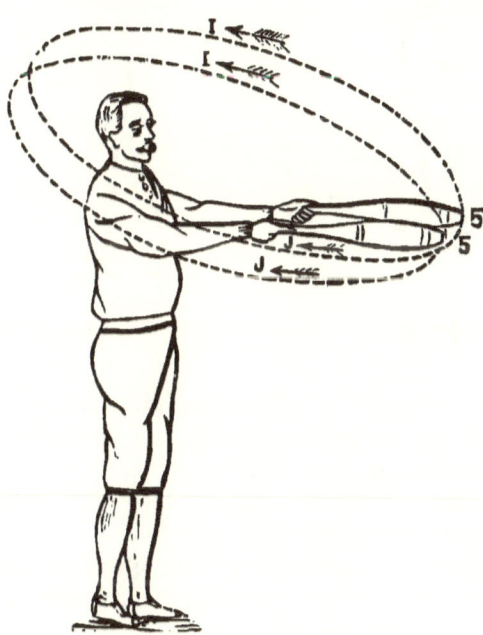

Fig. 5.

FOUR SIDE CIRCLES.

E.

From the first point of departure swing the left club directly forward, describing, on the left side of the body, several perfect straight-arm circles, cutting the plane of the front circles at right angles. Describe similar circles with the right club, moving directly forward on the right side of the body, also cut-

Fig. 6.

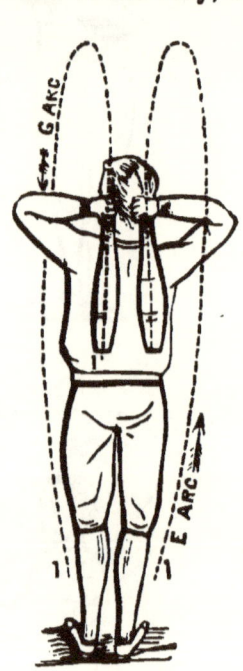

Fig. 7.

ting the plane of the front circles at right angles. As the club completes the first half of its course and enters the descending arc behind the shoulder, assist the movement by slightly swaying the body to the right or left, as the case may require. These circles are represented by the dotted lines and arrows in the ninth engraving. Describe with both clubs, allowing one of them to start half a revolution in advance of the other.

F.

From point **1,** swing the left club directly backward, describing a large side circle, assisting the movement by swaying the
body slightly to the left. Repeat, naming with each revolution
the distinctive letter F. Describe similar circles with the right

Fig. 8.

club, moving directly backward on the right side of the body
which sways to the right as the club ascends the arc. Endeavor
to keep the club, throughout the entire circuit, in the true plane
which crosses the floor line at right angles. (Eng. 9.) Describe
with both clubs, one following the other at half a circuit's
interval.

G.

Swing the clubs up the arc E to the second point of departure,
holding them perpendicularly at arms length above the head.

2*

From this point move the left club directly forward, describing several times a large straight-arm circle on the left side. Describe a similar circle with the right club, giving the distinctive name of the circle, G.

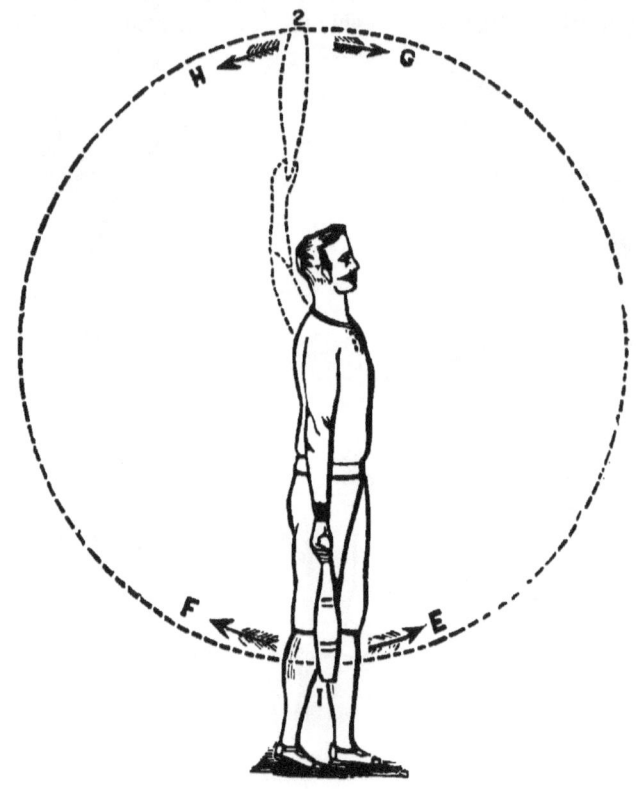

Fig. 9.

H.

From the same point 2, drop the left club backward describing H. The same with the right club. Practice the circles G and H with both clubs, one moving half a circumference in advance of the other, also both moving at the same moment in *opposite* directions, the left describing G and the right H, or vice versa. Try the same exercise from point 1, the left club describing E, and the right F, or vice versa. Favor the movements by swaying the person slightly to the right and left as each club passes to the rear. In these circles the clubs pass each other both at point 1 and 2. (Eng. 9.)

In this exercise it is allowable to change the position of the feet, by placing one twelve or fourteen inches in advance of the other, thus securing a brace, which is sometimes required when exercising with heavy clubs. (Eng. 10.)

Fig. 10.

TWO HORIZONTAL CIRCLES.

I.

Swing the clubs up on the arc E to a horizontal position, holding them straight out in front, at the height of the shoulders. This is the fifth point of departure, denoted by the numeral 5.

From this point swing the left club to the right, describing large circles in a horizontal plane directly over the head, associating with these circles the letter I. Describe similar circles by swinging the right club to the left in the same horizontal plane above the head. The tendency of the club to sink below the true horizontal plane at certain points of the circuit will be eventually overcome. (Eng. 5.) Describe with both clubs, each in turn tracing the upper curve.

J.

From the same point 5, swing the left club to the left and the right club to the right, describing large circles in the same horizontal plane above the head. These circles are denoted by J, and illustrated in the fifth engraving. The overhead horizontal circles have a diameter somewhat shorter than that of the front and side circles previously described, as the arm necessarily contracts a little as the club sweeps around back of the head. (Eng. 5.) Trace with both clubs.

TWO ELLIPTICAL CURVES.

It is proper to advert here to two elliptical movements which are described from the fourth point of departure, the clubs being held vertically in front of the breast, as shown in the fourth engraving. These curves bear a strong resemblance to the straight-arm circles C and D, but should be carefully distinguished from them. As the movement commences with the bent arm, the vertical diameter is shortened, producing an oblong figure instead of a perfect circle. From point 4, sweep the left club inwardly to the right just as in the circle C returning to the point of departure. Make the same movement with the right club moving to the left. Repeat the oblong several times with each club; then with both clubs moving alternately, the right starting on its circuit as the left returns, and the left starting again as the right returns. As each club comes in to its goal, bring it to a position just back of its mate with a quick arrest. (Eng. 4.)

To describe the second elliptical curve sweep the left club outwardly to the left just as in the circle D, returning to the point of departure. Make the same movement with the right club, moving outwardly to the right ; then, for an exercise, with both clubs moving alternately, the right starting out as the left returns, and the left moving out again as the right returns, both clubs moving in the same vertical plane. (Eng. 4.)

SECTION 2.

DORSAL OR BACK CIRCLES.

The dorsal circles are medium in size, and are designated by the letters **W, X, Y, Z.** The first two of these back circles are described from the first point of departure. In describing circles from this point, it is allowable, in starting, to swing the club gently in the direction opposite to the movement contemplated, in order to gain momentum to carry it up the ascending arc. In every circle there is a point of inertia to be overcome by imparting at the precise moment an additional impulse to the club. In circles made from the first point, this impulse is required at the start. In those emanating from the second, third and fourth points, it is not needed at starting, because the club immediately enters a descending arc, where its own weight affords sufficient momentum. In these cases the point of inertia being reached after the completion of the first semi-circle, the impulse must be imparted at that moment.

TWO LOWER DORSAL CIRCLES.

W.

Assume the appropriate attitude. From the first point of departure, throw out the left club to the left for a start; then carry it to the right, *behind the person*, causing it to describe a bent-arm circle in the rear. The club may be turned either by a flexible wrist movement, or by relaxing the grasp so as to allow the knob to turn in the hand, holding on principally by the muscles of the palm. The mode is immaterial so long as you succeed in making a smooth and even circuit. Describe the same circle with the right club moving first to the right for a start, then to the left, passing behind the person. Associate with these circles the significant letter **W**. (Eng. 11.) Turn this circle with both clubs, moving simultaneously.

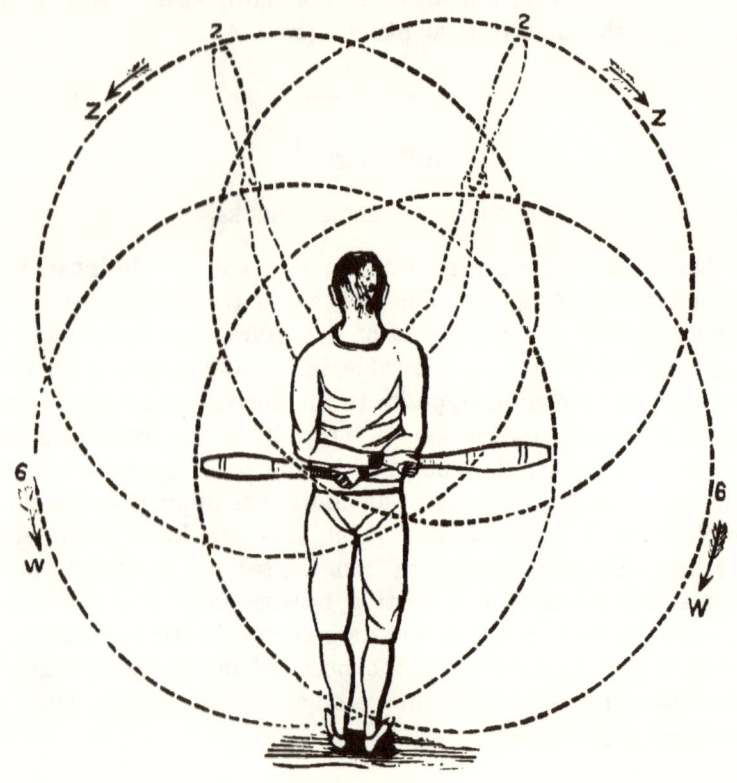

Fig. 11.

X.

The second lower dorsal circle denoted by **X,** more than any other, imperatively needs the aid of acquired velocity in order to ensure its smooth and graceful execution. For this reason it is usually made to follow a descending sweep of the club. From point **1** first impel the left club to the right for a start. As it returns, carry the hand quickly behind the hip, bending the arm and wrist so as to bring the head of the club nearly to the armpit as the hand passes behind. The acquired momentum, together with the sudden deflection of the arm from its previous course, causes the foot of the club to make a detour in the reverse direction to the preceding movement, amounting to a rear circle, to be associated with and designated by the letter **X**.

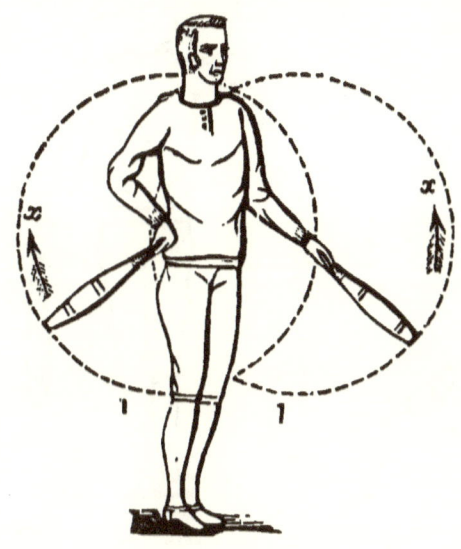

Fig. 12.

Describe the same circle with the right club moving first to the left for the sake of impetus. By practicing this circle in connection with, and following the front circle B, you will perceive at once how greatly accumulated momentum assists in turning it. The lower rear circles, alone, and disconnected from other motions are not repeated so readily as the upper; but alternating with other motions, as, for instance, the front circles A or B, or the front circlets p or q, the repeating movement soon becomes equally easy and natural, as will be made clearly apparent bye-and-bye. (Eng. 12.) Try with both clubs, in connection with the front circle B.

TWO UPPER DORSAL CIRCLES.

Y.

Swing the clubs up on the arc E to the second point, holding them perpendicularly at arm's length above the head. From this point carry the left club to the right *behind the shoulders*, causing it to describe a medium bent arm circle. Describe the same with the right club moving inwardly to the left. In this circle the point of inertia is reached just as the club enters the ascending arc of its circuit, and at this point an additional impulse must be imparted from the hand. Strive to carry the club

around evenly, adhering
to the true plane of the
circle, and allowing it
as long a diameter as
the bent arm will per-
mit. For an exercise
try this circle with both
clubs moving alternate-
ly; also with both
moving simultaneously.
Associate with this
movement the letter **Y**.
(Eng. 13.)

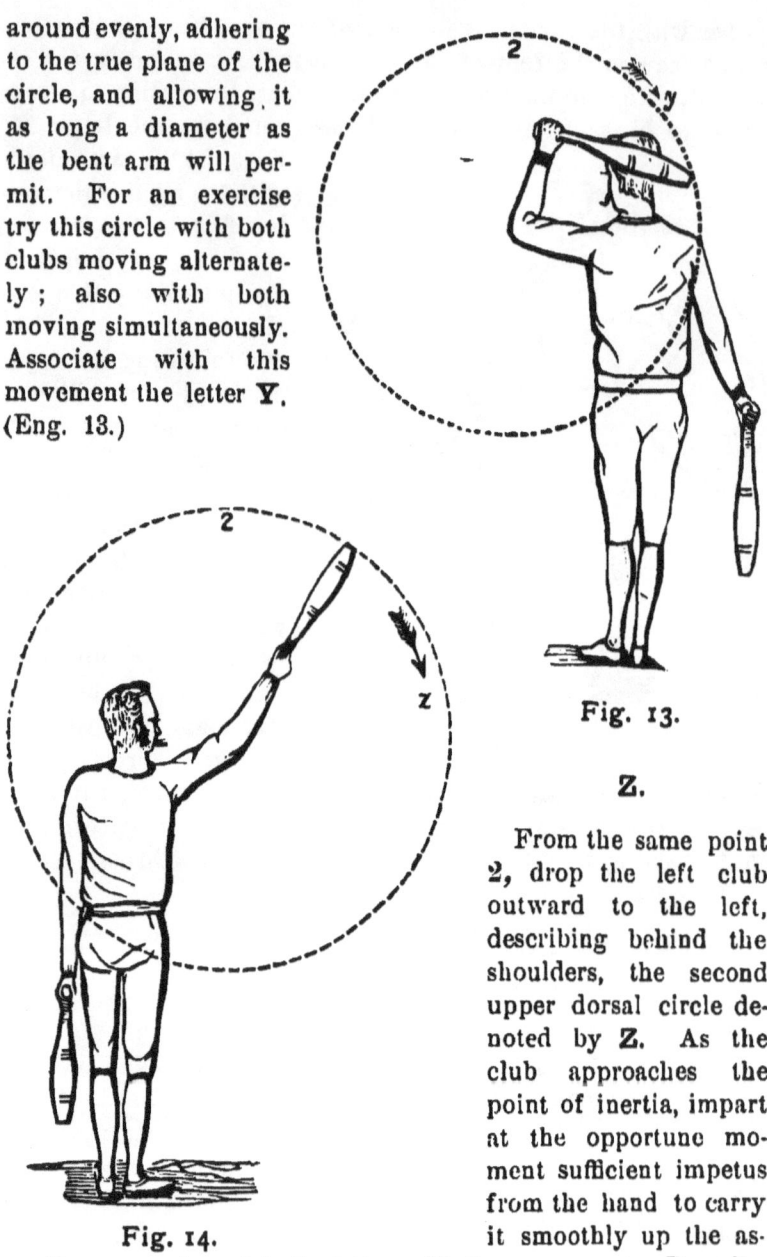

Fig. 13.

Z.

From the same point
2, drop the left club
outward to the left,
describing behind the
shoulders, the second
upper dorsal circle de-
noted by **Z.** As the
club approaches the
point of inertia, impart
at the opportune mo-
ment sufficient impetus
from the hand to carry
it smoothly up the as-

Fig. 14.

cending arc. Associate the letter with the movement. Describe
the same circle with the right club moving outwardly to the

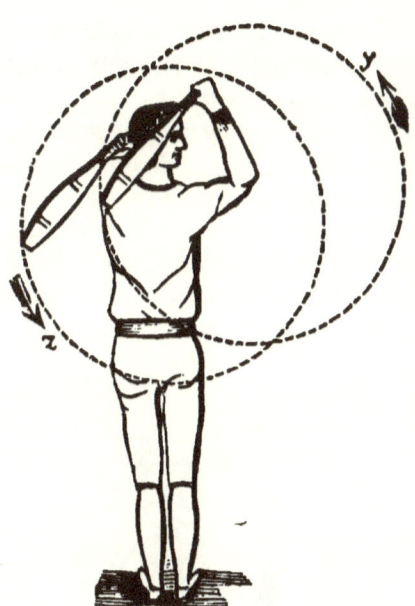

right. For an exercise, try both clubs, moving alternately. (Eng. 14.) Also both clubs moving simultaneously; and then both moving simultaneously in parallel circles, one describing the circle **Y**, and the other **Z**. (Eng. 15.) **Z** may be turned also from the first point of departure, by turning the arm back and forcing the club up the ascending arc.

Fig. 15.

SECTION 3.

EIGHT CIRCLETS OR WRIST CIRCLES.

These small circles, having for the most part a diameter only twice the length of the club, are numerous and are described in almost every plane, sometimes with straight, sometimes with bent arm, and at such height, angle or position as the swings to which they are attached may require. They are worthy of attention, because they serve to relieve the longer sweeps and diversify the movements, imparting to them the charm of variety, which is a desirable requisite both in mental and physical recreation. In fact,

" Variety's the very spice of life,
That gives it all its flavour."

The circlets which occur most frequently are the following:

1.

Swing the clubs up to a vertical position in front of the breast, which is the fourth point of departure, Press the left elbow

3

against the side, at the same time turning the wrist so as to throw
the thumb outwards. Drop the club directly forward, at the
same moment relaxing the grasp so as to allow it to turn freely
in the cavity between the thumb and forefinger, thus whirling
out, on the outside of the arm, a circlet, of which the wrist is
the centre of motion and the club the radius. The impelling
force is applied as the club enters the last half of its circuit.
Associate with this circlet the distinctive letter l. Whirl the
same repeatedly with the right club. (Eng. 16.) Also, with
both clubs: first, starting together; secondly, one starting half a
revolution ahead of the other.

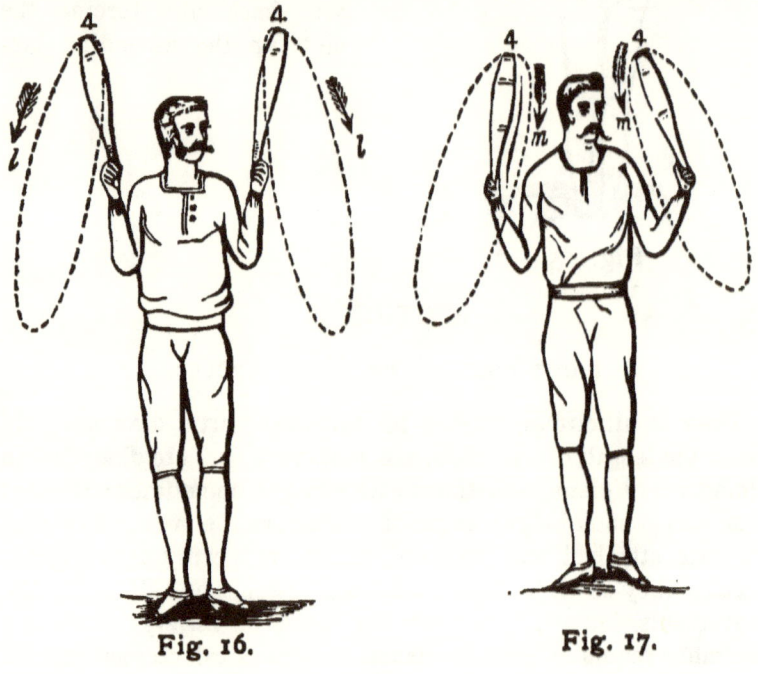

Fig. 16.   Fig. 17.

m.

From the same point, reverse the preceding movement, dropping the left club directly backward, on the outside of the arm,
whirling a circlet precisely like the first except being swept in
the opposite direction. The denoting letter is m. Repeat with
the right club. (Eng. 17.) Also, with both clubs: first, moving
together; secondly, one moving half a circle in advance of the
other.

n.

Straighten the elbows, holding the clubs vertically at arm's length, either in front or veering to either side. Send the left club forward, bringing it up this time on the inside of the arm. Denominate this circlet n, repeating the movement with the right club as usual. (Eng. 18.) Repeat also with both clubs.

o.

Reverse the preceding movement, sending the left club, from its vertical position, directly backward on the inside of the arm, producing the circlet o. Practice the same with the right club; (Eng. 18.) and simultaneously, with both clubs.

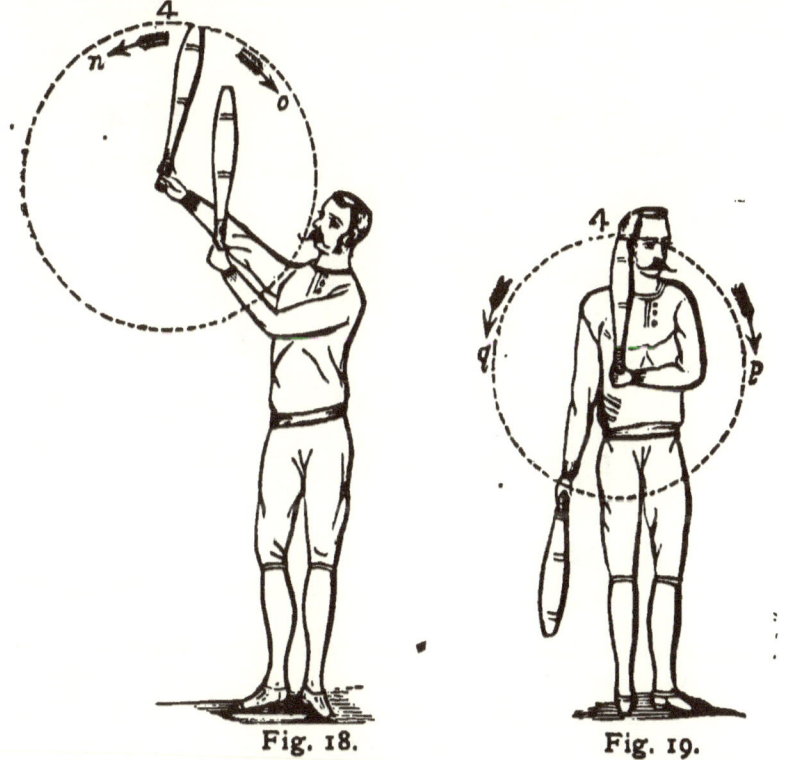

Fig. 18.   Fig. 19.

p.

Draw the arms back from the foregoing position, pressing the left forearm snugly to the body (the right club for the moment depending at the side). Starting the left club backward towards the elbow, relaxing the grasp and twisting the wrist so as to bring the thumb outward, whirl a circlet on the outside of the arm. Whirl the same with the right club (the left, for the moment, being dropped at the side,) the right forearm being pressed snugly to the body as the club drops backward towards the elbow. (Eng. 19.) As before remarked, these circlets are whirled from different positions, this one more frequently from the first point of departure. Practice p from the first point, the clubs moving in the plane of the great circles A and B. (Eng. 20.)

q.

Resume the position in front of the breast. Pressing the left forearm snugly to the body (the right club being dropped at the

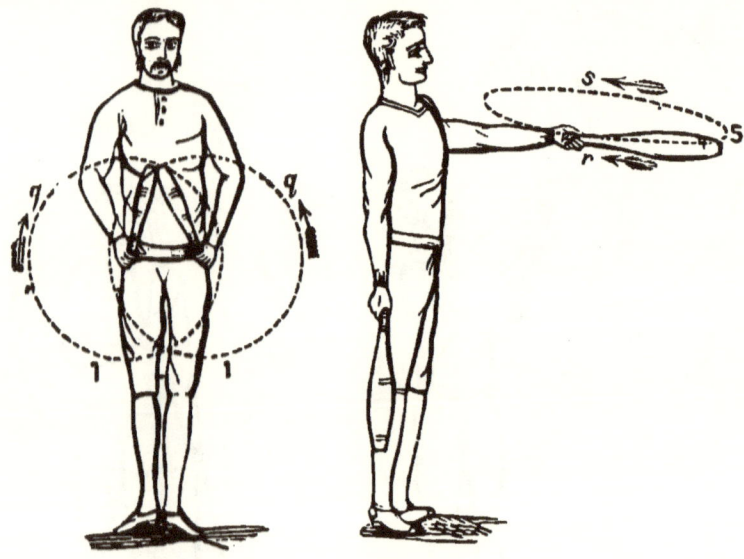

Fig. 20. Fig. 21.

side,) whirl a circlet, starting the left club forward in the reverse direction to the preceding movement, bringing it up on the outside of the arm. Repeat with the right club. (Eng. 19.) Practice q also from the first point. (Eng. 20.)

r.

Bring the clubs to point 5, holding them horizontally at arm's length in front, at the height of the shoulders. Whirl a circlet

by revolving the left club inwardly to the right, by flexure of
the wrist, the entire revolution being in front of the body and in
a perfectly horizontal plane above the arm. Repeat with the
right club revolving to the left. (Eng. 21.)

s.

From the same point, whirl a circlet with the left club revolving outwardly to the left in the same horizontal plane over the
arm; also with the right club revolving to the right. (Eng. 21.)

The beginner is not expected to make all these circlets with
perfect ease and smoothness at first. Expertness of movement
is the result of persistent effort. The raw mechanic handles the
implements of his trade clumsily enough at first; by and by, he
uses them as deftly as his fingers. The skilful feats of the expe-
rienced club-swinger excite wonder. Half an hour's daily practice will enable *you*, in a year or so, to exhibit the same feats.
The true object of club-swinging, however, is healthful exercise
rather than athletic display.

In this book precedence is uniformly given to the left arm,
which in most persons is weaker than the right in consequence
of neglect and disuse. By giving it the laboring oar, it soon at-
tains almost equal vigor and dexterity; striving nobly with the
right to secure for its master, the "inestimable wealth of health,
till he becomes, at length, erect, broad-chested, muscular, vigorous, healthy, happy, buoyant, victorious."

SECTION 4.

ARCS OF CIRCLES.

Arcs, or portions of the circumference of circles frequently
enter into the composition of swings. They are usually designated by the letters denoting the circles of which they form a
part. When it is unnecessary to indicate the direction of the
sweep, they may be referred to simply as front arcs, side arcs, etc.

FRONT ARCS.

Swing both clubs up to point 3 on the left side, holding them
parallel at an angle of forty-five degrees above the horizontal

3*

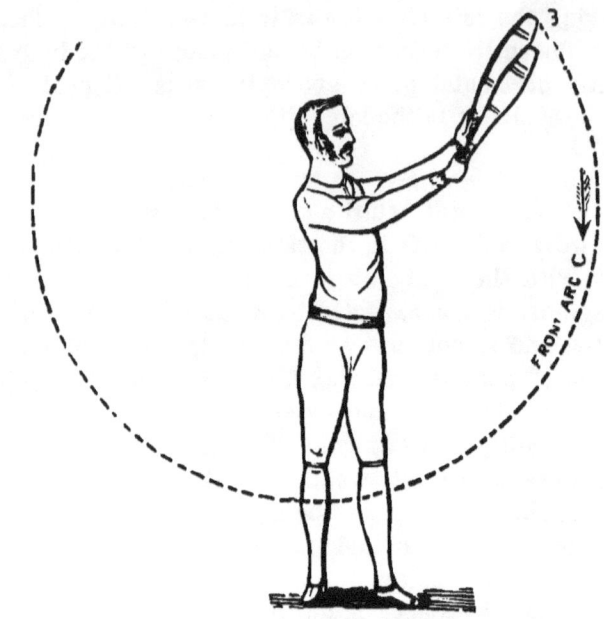

Fig. 22.

Fig. 7.

line of the shoulders. From this point swing them to and fro on the front arc, carrying them well up on each side so as to include nearly three-fourths of the entire front circle. Hold the clubs exactly parallel, both as they leave the point of departure and as they approach the corresponding point on the opposite side. (Eng. 22.)

SIDE ARCS.

Swing the left club up on the arc E allowing it to pass over the left shoulder, hanging vertically downwards. Return on the same arc, allowing the club to swing beyond the starting point 1, as far as the arm will permit. Repeat with the right club, then with both. (Eng. 7.)

For an exercise start the clubs from opposite points, the left from the first goal and the right from the position behind the shoulders. As the left swings forward and ascends the arc E, the right comes over the shoulder and descends the same arc. As the left descends on the return sweep, the right ascends and resumes its position behind the shoulder, which is an occasional point of departure, denoted by the numeral 7. (Eng. 7.)

HORIZONTAL ARCS.

Extend the left club horizontally at arm's length, on the left side, at the height of the shoulders; also the right club on the right side, at the same height. From these points swing them

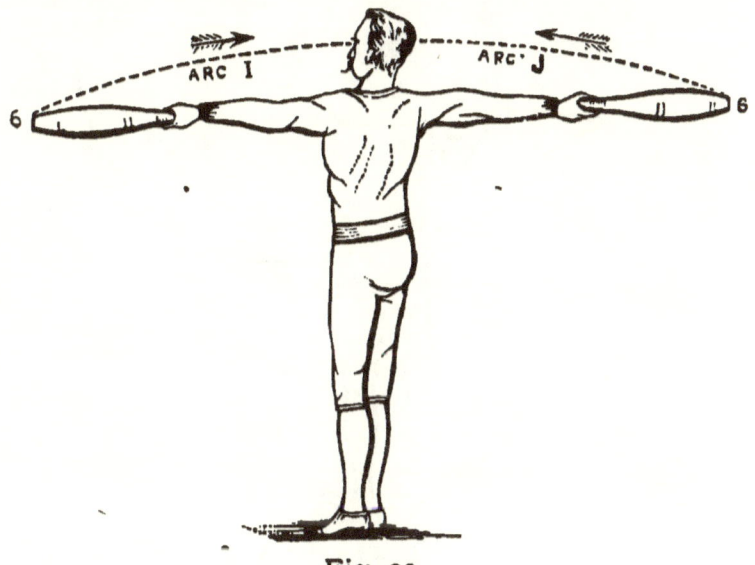

Fig. 23.

simultaneously back and forth on a horizontal arc, turning the body at the waist as far as possible without changing the position of the feet. (Eng. 23.) The above starting points are denoted by 6.

DORSAL ARCS.

From point 1, swing the left club gently to the right for a start, then to the left, passing it behind the left shoulder, and over the right shoulder and the head, returning by the arc in front. Repeat with the right club, moving first to the left for a

start, then to the right, passing behind the right shoulder and
over the left shoulder and the head, returning by the arc in front.
Also, for an exercise, extend both clubs horizontally at arm's
length on the left side, holding them parallel at the height of the
shoulders. From this point swing them around behind the
shoulders on a horizontal arc, returning by the arc in front.
Also start the clubs from the corresponding point on the right
side, traversing the horizontal arc behind the shoulders, and returning by the arc in front. (Eng. 24.)

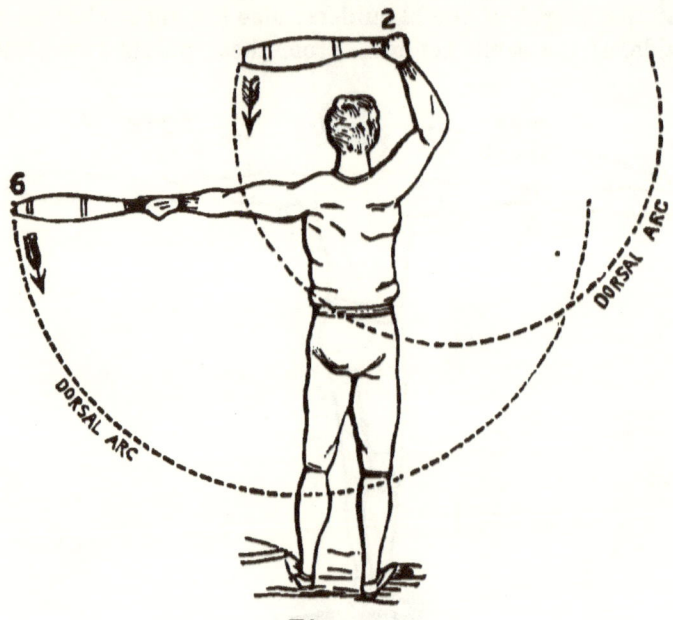

Fig. 24.

Secondly. Swing both clubs up to a horizontal position on
the left side, holding them parallel at the height of the shoulders
as before. Turn the left club back over the left shoulder, allowing it to traverse the dorsal arc and pass over the head, while at
the same moment the right club traverses the arc in front; as the
clubs reach a corresponding position on the right side, turn the
right club back over the right shoulder to traverse the dorsal arc,
while the left, dropping in front of the face sweeps the arc in
front, and so on continuously.

Thirdly. Raising the clubs to the same position on the left

side, parallel, at the height of the shoulders, turn the right club back, on the dorsal arc behind the right shoulder, and at the same moment, with the left club sweep the arc in front, bringing both clubs to a corresponding position on the right side; then turn the left club back on the arc behind the left shoulder while the right club sweeps the arc in front, and so on continuously.

Fourthly. Swing the left club back and forth on the dorsal arc and at the same time the right club back and forth on the front arc, counting the time 1. 2. : then the right club on the dorsal arc and the left on the front arc, and so on alternately.

The chief sources of health and longevity are diet, air, exercise and tranquillity. These conditions are pithily expressed in the following aphorism:

" Th' ingredients of health and long life are
Great temperance, open air,
INDIAN CLUBS, little care."

CHAPTER II.

·

DIVISIONAL STRUCTURE OF SWINGS.

Ordinarily, in exercising with the Indian Clubs, both hands are employed and participate equally in the movements. This circumstance imparts to each swing a two-fold or divisional character, the movements made with the left club constituting one division and similar movements with the right club, the other. These divisions are commonly united in two ways, expressed in the formulas by the initial letters (F) and (S). The first mode of union, denoted by (F) occurs when the left club executes the first movement of the swing while the right executes the second. The second mode of union occurs, when both clubs execute simultaneously each movement of the swing in succession.

Frequently the clubs are required to move in concert, describing parallel circles or arcs on one side of the person. Sometimes also, instead of moving strictly in concert, one club follows the other at an interval of half a circle. In these cases each division of the swing comprises the actions of both clubs and the union consists in repeating the same movements an equal number of times on the other side. This third method of uniting the divisions of which a swing is composed is expressed in the formulas by (T).

It is well to remember the divisional structure of swings, and in the first and second forms, to practice each division separately before uniting them to complete the swing. Even in the third form, clearer insight and greater facility of execution will be attained by resolving the swing into its elements and requiring each hand to do its work apart from the other.

The formula placed over the description of each swing indicates the movements composing it; the order in which they are
executed; the manner in which the divisions are united; and the
points from which the start is taken.

SECTION 1.

SWINGS COMPOSED OF TWO CIRCLES.

1.

1 G. (F.) 2.

The formula indicates that this swing is composed of the forward circlet 1, followed by the forward side circle G; that the
two parts of the swing are united by the first method; and that
the movements emanate from the second point of departure.

Fig. 25.

Refer back to the manual of single movements, if necessary, in order to refresh your memory in relation to these circles. This being done, swing both clubs up by the arc E to the second point of departure. (These points are often called goals.) From this point, whirl the circlet with the left club, and immediately after, without any pause in the movement, the large forward side circle. These two movements constitute the left division of the swing. The same movements made with the right club form the right division. Practice with each club until the transition from the small circle to the large and from the large to the small becomes easy and natural. Now complete the swing by uniting the two component parts according to the first method, as follows: Both clubs starting at the same momemt, each from its own goal, the left club whirls the circlet, while the right sweeps the large circle; then the left sweeps the large circle while the right whirls the circlet. Favor the long sweeps by swaying the body from side to side as the swing proceeds. (Eng. 25.)

The element of correct time is indispensable in club-swinging and should receive careful attention from the beginning of your practice. Each movement of the club should be measured and regular as the swinging of a pendulum. Be careful also to assume and adhere to the correct working attitude, keeping the body perfectly erect, knees straight, and toes turned out, as explained in the introduction.

The above swing is often varied by increasing the number of circlets. For example, add two more circlets to each division. Then the left club will turn three 1's while the right club turns two 1's and G; and when the left turns two 1's and G, the right turns three 1's. Practice this variation occasionally for a change.

Formula for the left club 1 1 1)
     "   "   "   right "   1 1 G)(F) 2.

2.

p A. (F.) 1.

This formula indicates that the swing is composed of a small and a large circle; also that the small circle precedes the large; that the two parts of the swing are joined by the first method, and that the goal or starting point is the foot of the club as it hangs by the side.

Starting the foot of the left club to the right from goal 1, whirl the circlet p, sweeping, instantly after, the large straight-arm front circle A. (For a particular description of these circles refer to the manual.) These two movements form the left division of the swing, the same movements made with the right club, from the right goal, forming the right division. Practice each division separately and then unite them by the first method,

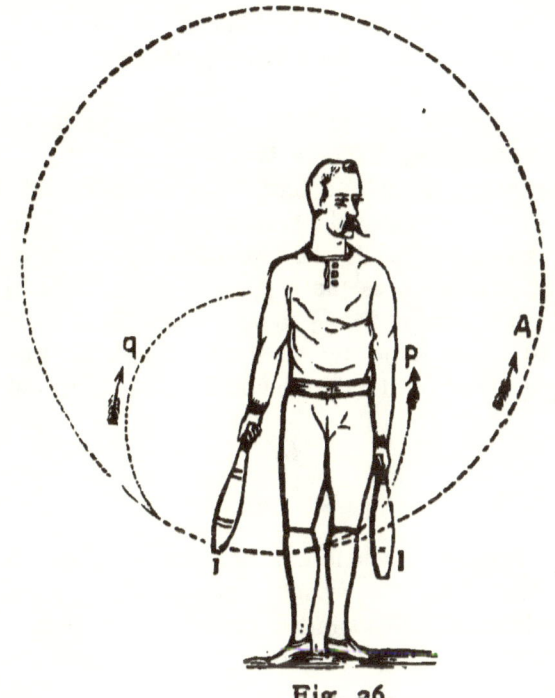

Fig. 26.

thus. Both clubs moving at the same moment, while the left turns the circlet p, the right sweeps the great circle A ; and when the left sweeps A, the right.reverts to p. (Eng. 26.)

<h2 style="text-align:center">3.</h2>

<h2 style="text-align:center">p A. (S.) 1.</h2>

This swing consists of the same circles swept from the same points, and in the same order. The divisions are the same, but they are joined together by the second method, which produces

4

from the same elements quite a different swing. Starting both clubs from point 1 at the same moment, whirl both circlets simultaneously and then both large circles. As the clubs pass in front, assign the outside circuit to each in turn. (Eng. 26.)

4.

q B. (F.) 1.

The circles of this formula are described in the same plane as those of the two formulas immediately preceding, but the sweeps of the club are reversed. The left club moving to the left from the first goal, whirls the circlet q, followed promptly by the straight-arm circle B. These two movements form the first half of the swing, the second half being composed of the same movements made by the right club moving to the right. After practicing separately, unite the two parts by the first method, the left club turning q as the right makes the large circle B : then, as the left sweeps the B, the right reverts to q. The circlet is turned by an impulsive wrist movement, the knob of the club being grasped by the thumb and fingers. (Eng. 26.)

5.

q B. (S.) 1.

In this swing the divisions are the same as in No. 4, but the union is effected by the second method, which requires both clubs to whirl simultaneously the circlet q, and then to follow with the large circle, each club in turn taking the outer circuit. (Eng. 26.)

6.

p D. (F.) 3.

In this light and airy swing, the circlet p is whirled at arm's length at the side, on the inside of the arm, the club being held by the thumb and fingers. When whirled from this point p coincides with n. Throw the left club up to goal 3, holding it at arm's length at an angle of forty-five degrees above the horizontal line of the shoulders. Whirl the circlet, the club passing at once, at this identical point, into the circumference of the straight-arm circle D, the two movements forming the first division of the swing.   Throw the right club up to the third goal on the right side, whirling the circlet and sweeping the circle from this point, these movements forming the second division.   After drilling on each division separately, unite the two

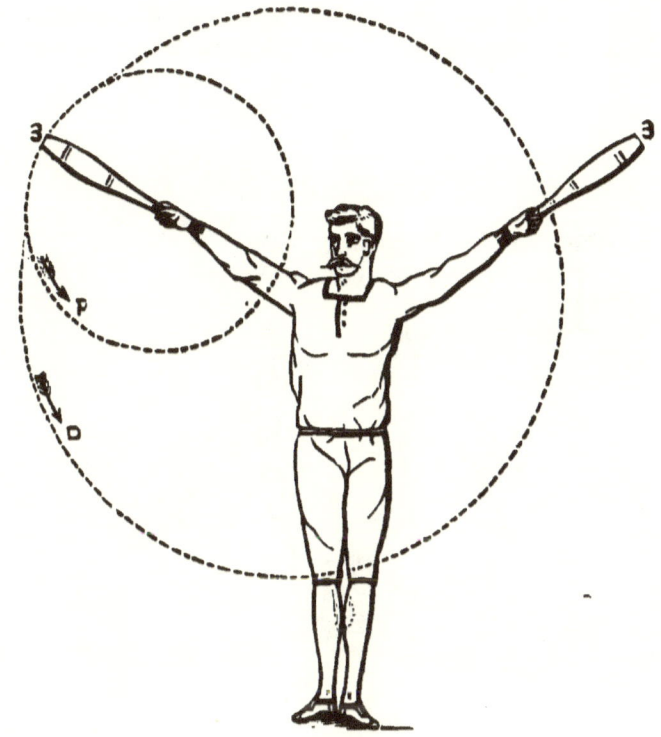

Fig. 3.

parts by the first method, the left club whirling the small circle while the right sweeps the large and vice versa.   Discontinue or prolong the movement at pleasure.   (Eng. 3.)   When a swing is undertaken for the purpose of learning it, it is well to adhere to the exercise with somewhat greater pertinacity than will be required after the movement has been thoroughly mastered and long familiarity has rendered it easy and natural.

7.

p D. (S.) 3.

Swing both clubs up to goal **3**, each on its own side of the person, holding them at arm's length at the angle before mentioned.   From these points whirl simultaneously with both clubs the circlet **p**, from which the clubs pass, without pausing, into the large front circle D, each in turn taking the outside circuit, as long as the swing continues.   (Eng. 3.)

8.

Y C. (F.) 2.

Swing the clubs up to goal **2**, either by the arc E or B. Drop the left club inwardly to the right, tracing a bent-arm cir-

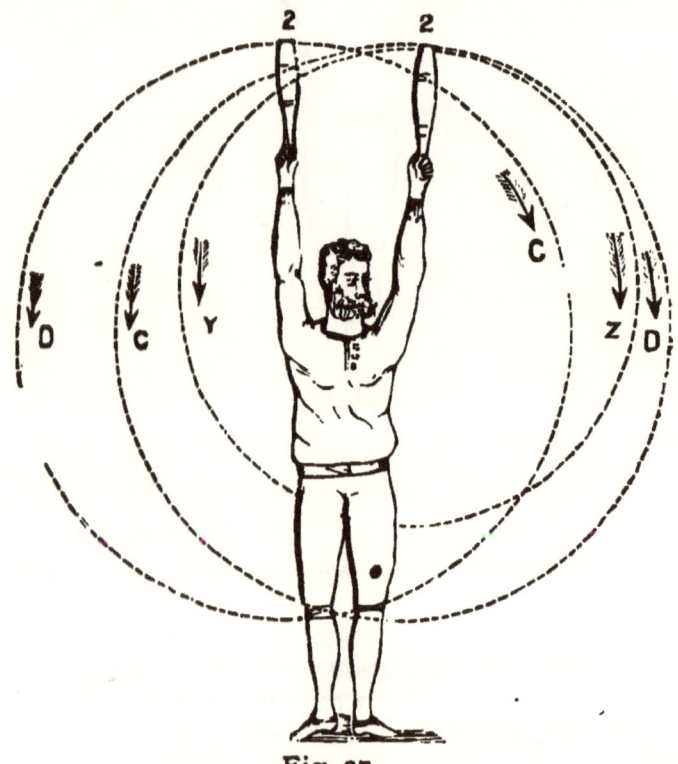

Fig. 27.

cle behind the head and shoulders, which is the first upper dorsal circle described in the manual. On the completion of this
circle, the club makes no pause, but continues right on into the
straight-arm front circle C, completing the sweep. These movements constitute the left half of the swing, the same movements
executed by the right club constituting the second or right half.
Practice separately, and then unite by (F). Both clubs moving
simultaneously, the left traces the back curve while the right
traces the front; and conversely the left traces the front, while
the right traces the back. Make full, free circuits behind as well
as in front, sinking the clubs well down as they pass the shoulders, thus granting to the dorsal curve as long diameter as the
bent arm will permit. (Eng. 27.)

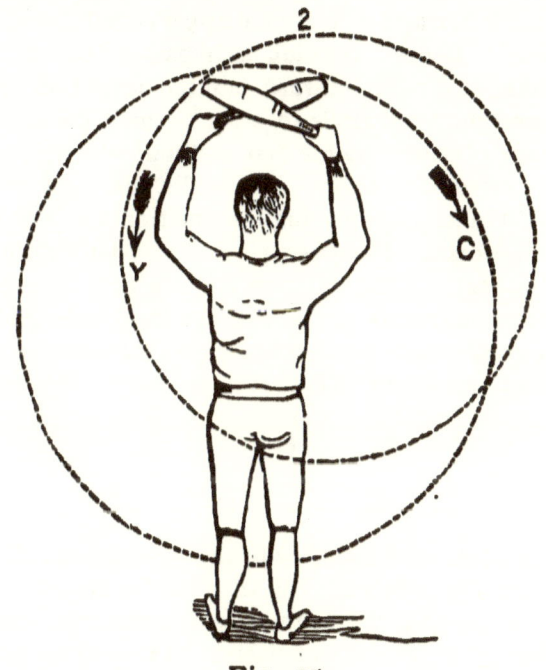

Fig. 35.

9.

Y C. (S.) 2.

From the same goal or starting point, unite the two divisions
according to the second method, the result being a swing wholly

4*

different in appearance, and bringing into action a different set of muscles. The clubs starting at the same instant cross first behind the head as they turn the double dorsal and again in front as they sweep into the straight-arm circles. It adds to the symmetry of the swing if each club is made to assume the outer circuit in turn, both in the back and front sweeps, but if found too difficult at this stage of your career, this point may be waived till a subsequent period of the course. (Engs. 27 and 35.)

10.

Z D. (F.) 2.

The point of departure is again at 2. Drop the left club outwardly to the left, tracing the second upper dorsal circle described in the manual. Depress the club as it passes behind the shoulders, sweeping it directly onward into the outer front circle D, the dorsal and the front circle together forming the first division of the swing. Connect by the first method, which requires the left club to sweep the dorsal circle while the right sweeps the front circle; the left club passing into the front circle as the right reverts to the dorsal. Practice well each division before attempting to unite them. Make full, free circuits both front and rear, with smooth continuous movement, the less circle gliding into the greater at the convenient point where the contours unavoidably approach and blend. (Eng. 27.)

11.

Z D. (S.) 2. (Engs. 27 and 36.)

The union of the two divisions by the second method produces a swing essentially different, both in muscular action and in visual effect. From goal 2 turn the dorsal circle with both clubs, followed promptly by the front circles. As the clubs sweep past each other above the head, in front, carry them well out to the right and left in order to afford ample scope and plenty of searoom, in which to repeat the double dorsal. (Eng. 36.)

This swing expands the chest and braces back the shoulders finely. It also invites repose.

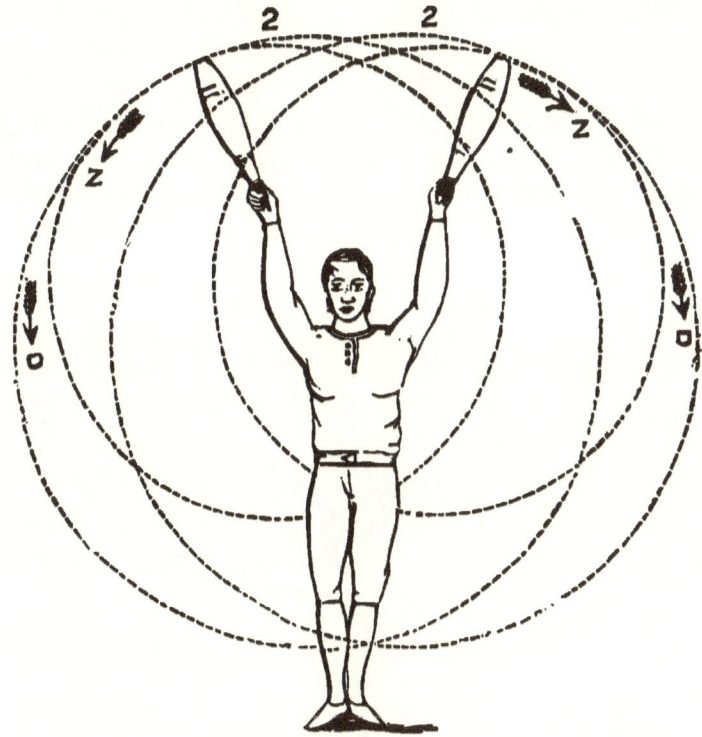

Fig. 36.

The potency of the exercise with the Indian clubs in inducing sleep, is beautifully symbolized in the legend of Kwasind, the strong man, by Longfellow.

> " To his ear there came a murmur
> As of waves upon a sea-shore,
> As of far-off tumbling waters,
> As of winds among the pine-trees;
> And he felt upon his forehead
> Blows of little airy war-clubs,
> Wielded by the slumbrous legions
> Of the Spirit of Sleep, Nepahwin;
> As of some one breathing on him.
>   At the first blow of their war-clubs,
> Fell a drowsiness on Kwasind;
> At the second blow they smote him,
> Motionless his paddle rested;
> At the third, before his vision
> Reeled the landscape into darkness,
> Very sound asleep was Kwasind."

12.

Y G. (F.) 2.

From goal 2 describe the inner dorsal Y with the left club, which passes at once into the large circle G, the two movements making the first division of the swing; the same movements

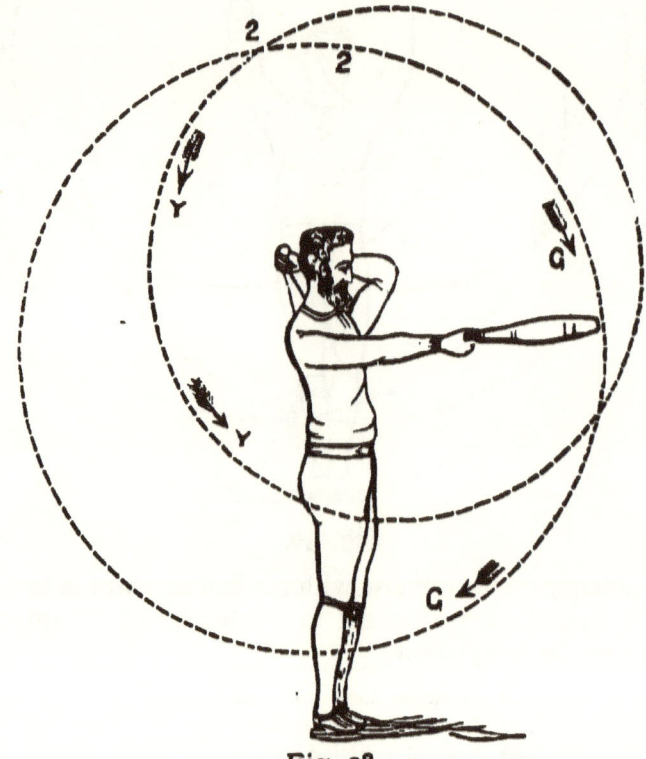

Fig. 28.

made with the right club form the second division. Connect them by (F.) In this swing, the union of the two divisions by (S) should not be attempted, as it subjects the shoulder joints to too severe a test. (Eng. 28.)

13.

r I. (F.) 5.

Raise the clubs to goal 5, holding them horizontally in front, at the height of the shoulders, at arm's length. Cause the left club, moving to the right, to revolve above the left arm, in a perfectly horizontal plane, describing the circlet r, which has for a radius the length of the club only, the entire circlet being swept in front of the person; then immediately after, sweep the club inwardly to the right again, describing the large circle I in the horizontal plane over the head, half the circuit lying in front of the head and half behind it. After practicing the divisions

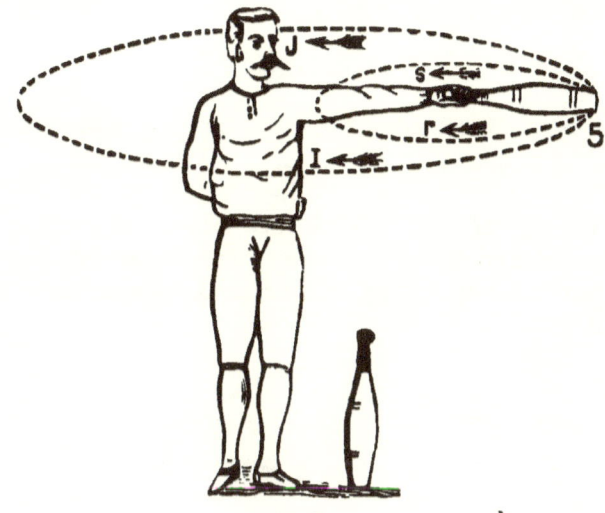

Fig. 29.

separately, unite them by (F), the left club revolving on the wrist as on a pivot, while the right sweeps the entire circuit, front and back, over the head. As the left movement expands into the large circle, the right contracts into the small. Confine the clubs strictly to the horizontal plane, a task requiring, at first, special effort on the part of the performer. (Eng. 29.)

14.

r I. (S.) 5.

Unite the two divisions by the second method, by causing both clubs, first, to revolve on the wrist as on a pivot describing r, and secondly, to sweep the large circle I at arm's length over the head. (Eng. 29.)

15.

s J. (F.) 5.

From the same goal, cause the left club to revolve to the left, first, in the small and then in the large circumference; also the right club to revolve to the right, first, in the small and then in the large circuit; unite the divisions by (F). (Eng. 29).

16.

s J. (S.) 5.

Work both clubs simultaneously, turning both outwardly, first, on the circlet and then on the circle, repeating at pleasure. (Eng. 29.)

The diameter of the overhead horizontals is of necessity somewhat shorter than that of the other large circles, in consequence of the unavoidable bending of the arm as the club passes behind the head.

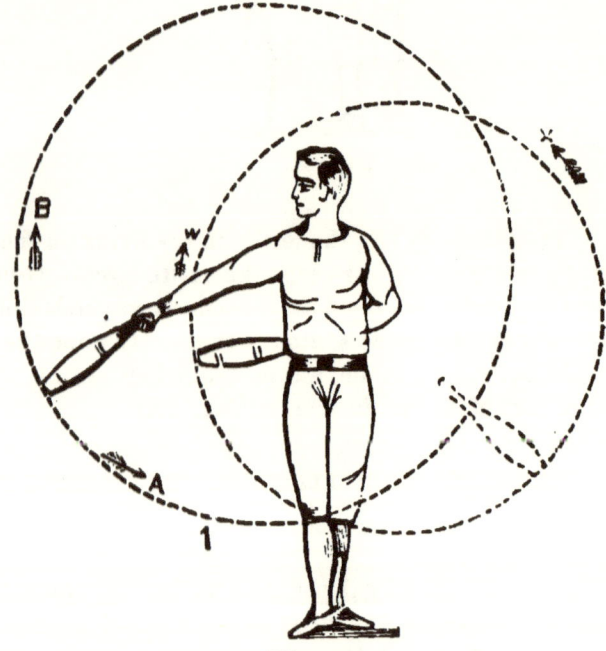

Fig. 30.

17.

A W. (F.) 1.

The left club moving to the right sweeps, from the first goal, the large straight-arm circle A in front, after which it passes, almost without change of direction, back of the person, where it describes the first lower dorsal circle W, the two movements forming the first half of the swing. The same movements repeated with the right club form the second half. Make the connection by (F), the left club sweeping in front, while the right turns at the back, and vice versa. In turning the lower dorsal relax the grasp, retaining hold on the button of the club chiefly by the muscular contraction of the palm of the hand. The working of the head of the club in the hand is somewhat after the manner of a ball and socket joint. (Eng. 30.)

18.

A W. (S.) 1.

Unite the divisions by (S), both clubs moving on A, and then both on W. The swing is rendered more symmetrical if each club in turn is made to take the outer circuit, both front and rear, but this point is not pressed at present. The art of turning the rear circles simultaneously without contact of the clubs is soon acquired. (Eng. 30.)

19.

B X. (F.) 1.

The left club, moving outwardly to the left describes the front circle B, followed immediately by the second lower dorsal circle, denoted by X, and detailed at length in the manual. The force accumulated from the downward sweep of the large circle and the sudden change of direction suffice to cause the foot of the club to take a circular route behind the hip. Unite the divisions by (F). As the right club has no accumulated force to start with, it may be held in abeyance during the first movement by the left, or, the dorsal movement may be simply feinted. Momentum being an indispensable element in this dorsal circle, it should always be made to follow a descending sweep. (Eng. 30.)

20.

B X. (S.) 1.

Both clubs simultaneously sweep, first, the front circle B, and, secondly, the back circle **X,** repeating continuously. (Eng. 30.)

21.

B W̄. (F.) 1.

The left club moving to the left describes the large circle B. As the club goes past the person in front, let it swing beyond the goal to a horizontal point at the height of the shoulders,

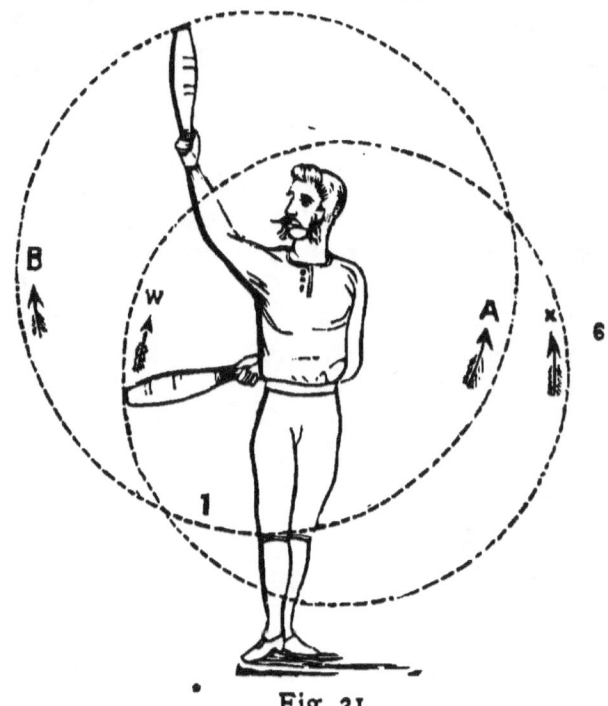

Fig. 31.

from which point it takes the opposite direction, describing the dorsal **W,** in the rear. These movements are the first division, the second being the same movements performed with the right club. Unite by (F). (Eng. 31).

22.

B W. (S.) 1.

Describe the front circle with both clubs. As they go past the person in front, allow them to swing beyond the goals till they reach a horizontal position on opposite sides, thus affording an opportunity for the free and graceful performance of the double dorsal W. (Eng. 31.)

23.

A X. (F.) 1.

With the left club moving to the right, describe the large front circle A. As the club descends, let it swing well past the goal in front of the person, preparatory to executing the lower dorsal X : then execute the dorsal as previously directed. These movements form the left division of the swing, the right division being formed of the same movements made with the right club. After separate practice unite the divisions by the first method. (Eng. 31.)

24.

A X. (S.) 1.

Unite the two divisions by the second method. First describe with both clubs the double front circle A, allowing the clubs to go well past the goals in front preparatory to turning the double dorsal. Then turn the double dorsal. Repeat several times. (Eng. 31.)

25.

Y 1. (F.) 2.

Swing the clubs up on the arc E or B to the second point of departure, holding them perpendicularly above the head. From this point the left club, moving to the right describes the upper dorsal Y, and immediately after from the same point the forward circlet 1. Make the union by (F). (Eng. 32.)

5

26.

Y 1. (S.) **2**.

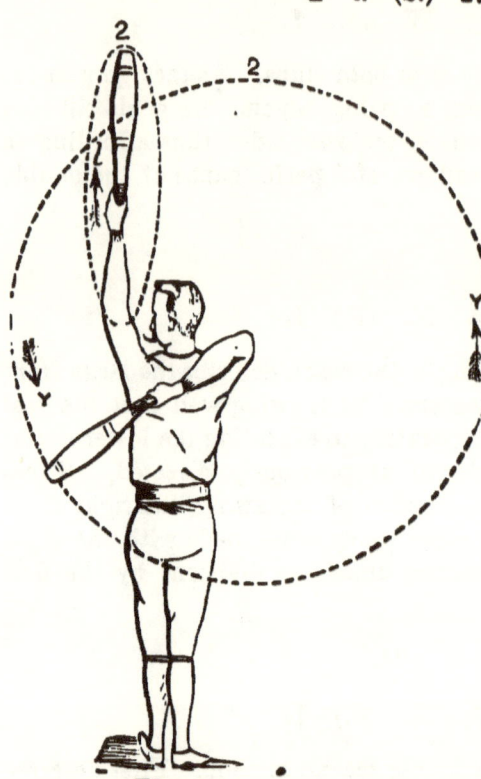

Fig. 32.

Unite the divisions by (S), executing first the double dorsal and then the double circlet. (Eng. 32).

27.

W Z. (F.) **1**.

This is an attractive formula, but requires both care and skill in the execution. Describe the lower dorsal **W**, impelling the left club first gently to the left and then to the right, turning the circle behind the hips. After making the turn bring the club quickly around in front of the person, and carry it up the front arc **A** to a point convenient for turning the left dorsal **Z**, which is then turned. The short arc in front, required to connect the lower back circle with the upper is not expressed in the formula, as it comes in of necessity, it being impossible otherwise to execute the swing. These several movements constitute the left section of the swing, the right section consisting of similar movements made with the right club. Practice each section thoroughly before attempting to unite them. The union is by (F). The left club turns the **W** below, while the right turns **Z** above, and when the left ascends the arc to perform the **Z**, the right descends to execute the **W**. In this, as in other swings involving the lower dorsal movement, the execution should be slow and deliberate. (Eng. 33)

28.

W   Z. (S).   **1.**

With both clubs moving simultaneously describe the dorsal
W: then bringing the clubs in front, carry them up the inner

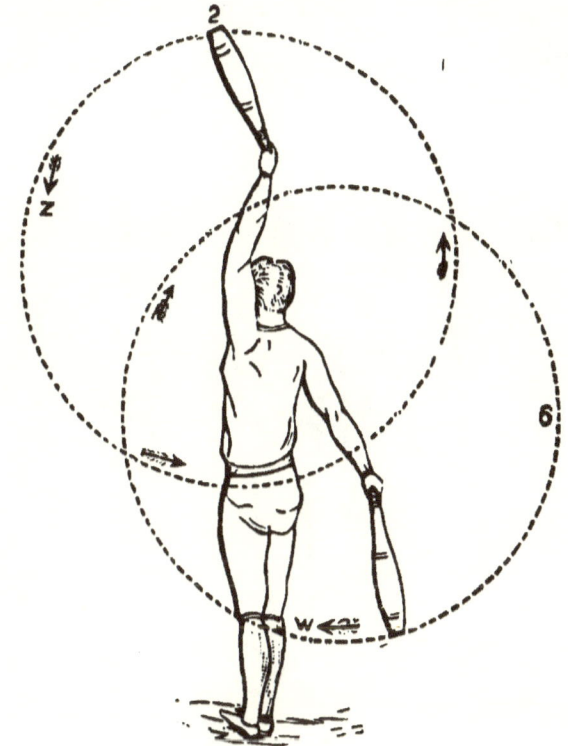

Fig. 33.

arc **A**, making a generous detour to the right and left so as to
allow the **Z** to be turned fairly and squarely in its own proper
place behind the shoulders.   In swings of this kind much of the
interest attached to them depends upon the style of execution.
The movements should never be hurried nor cramped, but on
the contrary quite moderate in point of time, and free and lib-
eral in point of space.   (Engs. 11 and 33.)

29.

Under this head are included several swings which are grouped
together on account of their similarity.   They are designed to

impart proficiency and skill in turning the lower back circles in connection with the circlets. The student should revert to them from time to time as he may find leisure and opportunity, some-

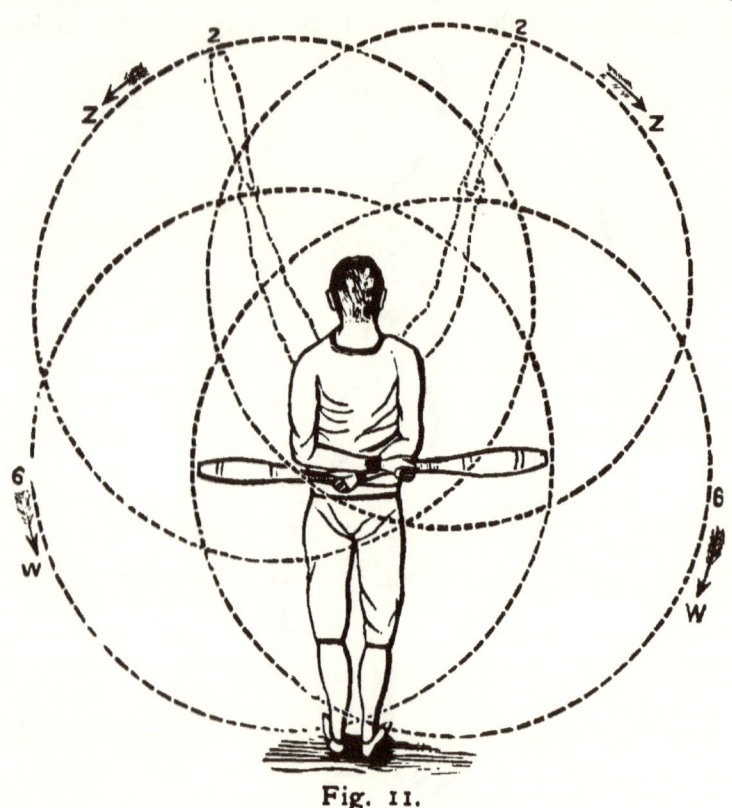

Fig. 11.

thing more than mere cursory and superficial practice being required to attain perfect ease and dexterity in turning these circles.

"He who would search for pearls must dive below."

The formulas are as follows:

1st.

p W. (F.) 1.

With an impulsive motion of the wrist turn the circlet p in front, in the plane of the great circle A, with the left club, and at the same moment the dorsal circle **W**, in the rear, with the right: then, changing duty, the left club turns the dorsal and the right the circlet. In turning the circlets, throw the clubs well out to the right and left in order to afford a straight sweep behind for the **W**. A finer bent-arm and wrist movement than this need not be desired.

2d.

p W. (S.) 1.

Unite the divisions also by the second method, first turning the p with both clubs, and then the **W**.

3d.

q W. (E.) 1.

Turn the circlet q with the left club moving outwardly to the left from the first goal, in the plane of the great circle B; at the same time turn the back circle **W** with the right club, also moving to the left. Then describe the dorsal with the left club and the circlet with the right. The movement is similar to that in No. **21**, the small circle q taking the place of the large circle B. Unite the divisions also by the second method, the formula being q **W**. (S.) **1**.

4th.

Left club 1 **W** }(T) 3.
Right " 1 q }

In this swing the point of departure for both clubs is goal 3 on the left side. From this point both clubs start at the same time and make as nearly as possible the same movements; q in front corresponding to **W** in the rear. These movements made on the left side with both clubs form the left division of the swing, and similar movements made with both clubs from goal 3 on the right side form the right division. The third method of union enunciated at the beginning of this chapter is applied in this case. Swing both clubs up to goal 3 on the left side. From this point, whirl the circlet 1 with both clubs, after which, both traversing the short intervening arc, the left club turns the lower dorsal **W** behind the hips, while the right turns the cor-

responding circle q in front. Now swing both clubs up to goal
3 on the right side, from which point both clubs turn the circlet
1, descend together the short intervening arc, the right passing
behind the hips and turning the dorsal while the left turns the
corresponding circle q in front. Thus the swing proceeds from
side to side, the clubs moving in concert till the close. The short
arc is disregarded in the formula, as it intervenes of necessity,
when the start is made from the third goal. Face to the left and
right as the clubs change from one side to the other, the body
turning at the waist.

5th.

$$\text{Left club } m \quad W \atop \text{Right ''} \quad m \quad q \Big\} (T) \ \mathbf{3.}$$

This formula differs from the preceding only in the substitu_
tion of the backward circlet m in place of the forward circlet 1.
When you turn the circlet m allow the clubs to drop back over
the shoulders, hanging vertically downwards; from this position
they are thrown forwards and turn the other circles precisely as
in the preceding swing.

6th.

$$\text{Left club } n \quad 1 \quad W \atop \text{Right ''} \quad n \quad 1 \quad q \Big\} (T) \ \mathbf{3.}$$

This formula requires two circlets to be turned at the start.
Turning the wrists to suit the movement, first let both clubs drop
forward and bring them up on the inside of the arms; then let
them drop forward again and bring them up on the outside of
the arms, after which complete the swing as before shown.

7th.

$$\text{Left club } o \quad m \quad W \atop \text{Right ''} \quad o \quad m \quad q \Big\} (T) \ \mathbf{3.}$$

Here the two backward circlets are turned at the start. Stretch-
. ing out the arms, let both clubs drop back on the inside of the
arms turning the circlet o ; then back on the outside, turning m,
at the same time throwing the clubs over the shoulders. The
remainder of the swing is like the preceding. (Eng. 34.)

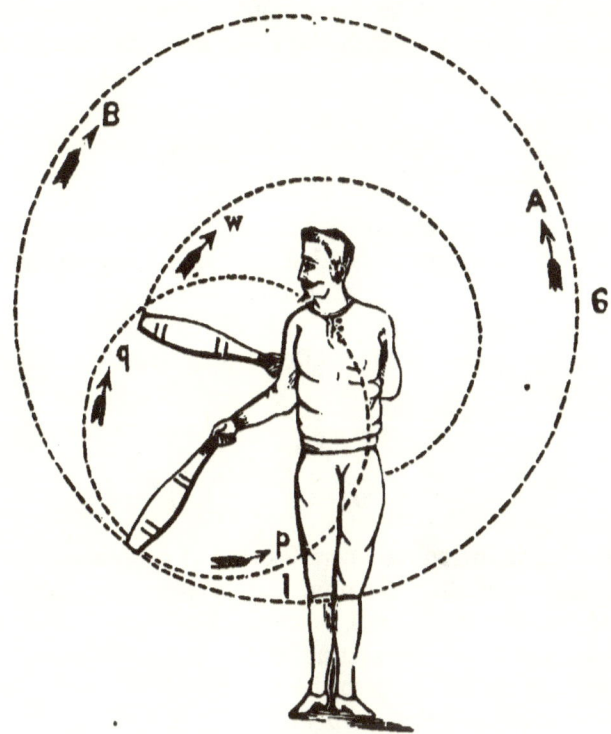

Fig. 34.

Similar formulas may be framed involving the second lower dorsal **X**, as follows:

1. p **X** (F) **1.**
2. q **X** (F) **1.**
3. Left club l p $\Big\}$(T) **3.**
    Right " l **X**
4. Left club m p $\Big\}$(T) **3.**
    Right " m **X**
5. Left club n l p $\Big\}$(T) **3.**
    Right " n l **X**
6. Left club o m p $\Big\}$(T) **3.**
    Right " o m **X**

Practice these formulas until they become quite familiar: also the following, in which the clubs describe two front and two back parallel circles.

$$\text{Left club q} \quad X \atop \text{Right " } \quad p \quad W \Big\} (T) \quad 1.$$

In turning the circlets throw both clubs well out to the right, which brings them into a parallel position at convenient points for describing the back circles, namely, X with the left club, and W with the right. From the back circles return promptly to the front, the clubs all the while turning parallel circles both front and rear.

30.

q B W A. (T.) 1.

This swing is introduced here because it contains some points of resemblance with those immediately preceding, although it contains four circles instead of two. The clubs move in concert throughout, only separating at the third movement, where the left passes behind to describe the dorsal W, while the right makes the corresponding turn in front, after which they rejoin and sweep together the final front circle. By an impulsive effort of the wrists, turn the circlet with both clubs, sweeping, directly after, the large front circle. As the clubs descend the arc on the right, allow them to swing past the goal to a horizontal position on the left. 'From this point, separating, the left club describes the dorsal W, while the right turns in front. Then joining again, both sweep in concert the large front circle A, which completes the left division of the swing. Applying the third mode of union, the second or right division is developed by repeating similar movements from the first goal on the right side, the clubs moving in concert throughout, separating at the third movement, of necessity, to allow the right club to describe the dorsal while the left turns in front. We have placed over this swing only the formula for the left club, as the right moves along with it all the way, turning corresponding circles. The formula for the right club would be p A q B. (Eng. 34.)

31.

p A X B. (T.) 1.

This exercise is similar to the preceding only involving the second lower dorsal circle **X**, in the place of **W**. The formula indicates the action of the left club, the right moving in concert and turning correlative circles. When the left club is required to turn the dorsal **X**, the right is occupied in whirling the circlet p in front. The formula for the right club would be q B p A. (Eng. 34.)

32.

p E. (F.) 1.

From point **1** sweep the large forward side circle **E** with the left club, on the left side of the body, and at the same moment with the right club whirl the corresponding small forward side

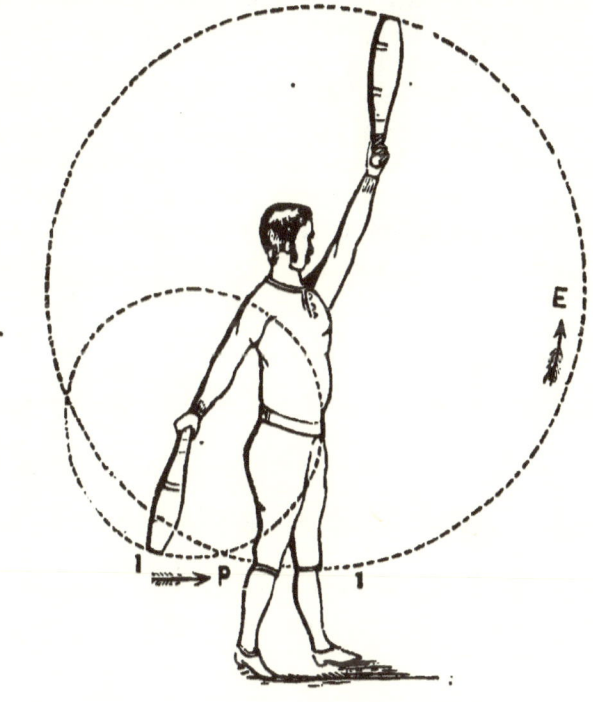

Fig. 44.

circlet **p** on the right side, each club alternating constantly from large to small and from small to large as the swing proceeds. Whirled from this point and on the side, p coincides with m. This movement being rather difficult may be omitted in the first course and taken in the review. (Eng. 44.) Vary this swing by increasing the number of circlets, thus:

$$\left.\begin{array}{l}\text{Left club } p \quad p \quad p \\ \text{Right } `` \quad\quad p \quad p \quad E\end{array}\right\}(F) \quad 1.$$

33.

Y X. (F.) 2.

From point 2 turn the back circle **Y** with the left club, while the right, descending the arc **C** in front gathers impetus to turn handsomely the lower dorsal **X**. The left club then descends the arc and turns the lower dorsal, while the right, ascending the arc **B** turns the upper dorsal **Y**. In the formula above given the arcs are not expressed, as the clubs must of necessity traverse them in passing from the upper to the lower circles. Considered as a swing composed of three movements, it might be formulated thus: **Y arc C X. (F.) 2.**

An interesting experiment may be tried here by executing consecutively two swings, the first of which contains the upper dorsal circles and the second the lower. Practice in this manner the following formulas, and other similar combinations as they may occur to you:

Y	C	(F)	2.	alternating with	Y	X	(F)	2.
Y	C	(S)	2.	"	"	Y	X	(S)	2.
Z	D	(F)	2.	"	"	Z	W	(F)	2.
Z	D	(S)	2.	"	"	Z	W	(S)	2.

"Young man, you look as if you were in trouble; are you sick?"

If so, try the Indian club treatment, called sometimes "the amateur's specific;" the uniform result of which may be expressed in three words,

"'Tis exercise and health and length of days."

Mark the three-fold beneficent result, exercise, health and longevity. Examples are not rare in which sickly and slender youths have been braced up by exercising with the clubs, becoming thoroughly hardened in a few years, and tough, nearly, as a Norwegian sailor,

> " Iron-sinewed, horny-handed,
> Shoulders broad, and chest expanded,
> Tugging at the oar."

SECTION 2.

SWINGS COMPOSED OF A CIRCLE AND AN ARC, OR OF TWO ARCS.

1.

As in No. 29 of the previous section, several swings, on account of their similarity, are here collected together under one head. The basis of each swing is the to and fro movement, in concert, of both clubs from the third point of departure on the left side to the corresponding point on the right side, from which they return again to the left. In these cases where the right club is thrown up to the goal on the left side in order to act in concert with the left, while the *movement* of the right club is the same as that of the left, the literal expression of the formula is different, arc D to the left club being arc C to the right, and q to the left, p to the right, and so of other circles in the same plane. It might perhaps be deemed sufficient in such cases to give the formula for the left club, remarking that the right moves in concert with it; but in order to prevent any misconception of the movements, I have preferred to give the formula for each club.

1st.

Left club 1 arc D } (T) 3.
Right "   1 arc C }

Throw both clubs up to goal 3, on the left side, holding them parallel at arm's length. Turn the circlet 1 with both clubs; then swing on the front arc to the corresponding point on the right side. Here repeat the circlets and return. (Eng. 22.)

2d.

Left club m arc D ⎫(T) 3.
Right "   m arc C ⎭

This swing is the same as the first, only substituting the backward circlet in place of the forward, allowing also the clubs to drop back over the shoulders.

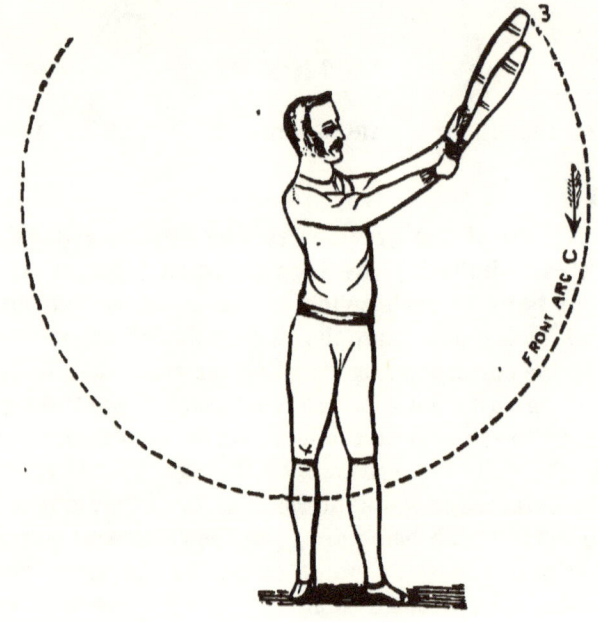

Fig. 22.

3d.

Left club n 1 arc D ⎫(T) 3.
Right "   n 1 arc C ⎭

Turn two circlets previous to sweeping the arc, first n, on the inside, then 1, on the outside, of the arms, both being forward circlets. (Eng. 22.)

4th.

Left club o m arc D ⎫
Right "   o m arc C ⎬ (T) 3.

Reverse the preceding circlets, extending the arms to allow
the clubs to turn safely towards the face. After turning the
circlets, drop the clubs back over the shoulders. In the four
swings now enumerated, the first division is the formula as executed from the point of departure on the left side, and the second as executed from that on the right side, the union being by
the third method explained at the beginning of the chapter. In
practicing swings of this kind, the clubs should be thrown well
up to the right and left, so as to embrace in each sweep about
three-fourths of the entire circle in front. The feet may retain
one position, the body turning at the waist; or occasionally, for
a change, you may turn on the feet, keeping them at right angles
as you face from the one side to the other.

Two variations of the first swing (1 arc D) may be described
here. The first consists in turning the circlets very low down on
the left side, sinking the clubs nearly to the floor; then as you
face to the right, turn the hands back so as to bring the clubs
behind the shoulders, throwing them to an extreme height; the
movement being uniformly depressed on one side and elevated
on the other as the swing proceeds.

The second variation consists in starting one club from a horizontal position and the other from behind the shoulders, the
second following the first at an interval. Face to the left, throwing the left club over the left shoulder, where it hangs pendent
behind. Extend the right club horizontally on the left side.
This is the position for starting; the left club being at goal 7 and
the right at goal 6. Turn the circlet 1 with the right club, which
is then swung across on the front arc C, and by a quick backward turn of the arm is thrown over the right shoulder, the body
meantime facing to the right. At the moment the right club
passes in front, make a high throw with the left from behind the
shoulder swinging it across on the front arc D to a horizontal
position on the right side, where it stops. Now the situation is
just the reverse of the original, the left club being extended horizontally on the right side, while the right depends from the right

6

shoulder, the body facing to the right. Repeat the movement as follows: The left club turns the circlet, traverses the arc and comes to position over the left shoulder; while the right, follow-lowing at an interval with a high throw, also traverses the arc, and stops at a horizontal position on the left, the body now fac-ing to the left. When thus facing the formula is

Left club   arc D starting from 7 stopping at 6.
Right "   1   arc C   "   from 6 stopping at 7.

2.

Left club 1 1 arc D
Right "   arc C arc D arc C ⎱ (T) 3.

Swing both clubs up to goal 3 on the left side, holding them parallel. First, turn the circlet 1 with the left club, while the right swings across on the arc C to a horizontal position on the right side at the height of the shoulders; secondly, turn the circ-let again with the left club while the right swings back on the arc to the original position; thirdly, swing both clubs on the arc to the third goal on the right side, these several movements be-ing the left division of the swing, the return movements forming the right division. Throw the clubs well up as they meet to traverse in company the final arc. (Eng. 22.)

This swing admits of two modifications. Make one circlet with the left club and a complete circle with the right, after which they swing together to the goal on the right. The form-ula becomes

Left club 1 arc D
Right "   C arc C ⎱ (T) 3.

The other modification consists in turning circlets, one above and one below the left arm, and then swinging together to the right side where the movement is repeated. Force the right club under the left arm, compelling it to make as nearly as possible the same turn under the arm as the left makes above it. The formula becomes

Left club 1 arc D
Right "   n arc C ⎱ (T) 3.

Try also the following exercise, which is somewhat similar: facing to the left, cross the arms at the breast and turn with both clubs the circlet n ; uncross quickly, turn 1 with both clubs swing across on the front arc and repeat.

3.

Y arc C arc D (F) 1..

The movements of the formula made with the left club are the first division; made with the right club, the second. Practice the divisions and unite them by the first method. The start is taken from the first point of departure. The analysis of the swing is as follows: The left club moving to the left, ascends the arc and turns the dorsal circle Y, while the right swings out to a horizontal position on the right at the height of the shoulders and back to a similar position on the left. Secondly, the left club, descending the arc C swings out to a horizontal position on the left and back to a similar position on the right, while the right club swinging back from the left side, ascends the arc on the right and turns the dorsal. The clubs pass each other exactly in front of the person, the descending club always taking the outer circuit. Swing with a steady, even movement, observing exact moderate time. On account of its easy cradle-like motion, this is sometimes called the sleepy swing.* It certainly exerts a soporific influence if long continued.

" Oh sleep! it is a gentle thing,
Beloved from pole to pole!"

Vary the above swing by substituting the dorsal arc Z, now and then for the circle Y, the club returning by the arc C in front. Vary also by introducing occasionally the double front circle B, reverting again to the original movement. These substitutions prevent the swing from seeming monotonous and at the same time afford relief to the arms by change of motion.

The above swing may be increased in volume, without marring its individuality by turning the dorsal three times in succession, at the same time increasing the number of arc sweeps correspondingly. Try the experiment.

---

* The sobriquet of each leading swing is given in the table of contents at the end of the book.

4.

Y   arc C   arc D   (S)   1.

From goal **1,** the left club moving to the left and the right club to the right, both ascend the arc and turn the dorsal **Y**; then descend on the arc C, swinging out to a horizontal position on opposite sides, whence they return to an opposite horizontal position, the arms being crossed upon the breast. From this latter position the swing is repeated. The clubs intersect four times, first behind the shoulders, then above the head in front, and twice below as they pass out *to* the side points and return *from* them. For diversification, the simultaneous **Y** turns in this swing may occasionally be made at arm's length, at goal **3.**

5.

Z   arc D   arc C   (F)   1.

After practicing the divisions, unite by the first mode, the ascending club always taking the outside circuit. The analysis is as follows: While the left club, moving to the right, ascends the arc, sweeping gracefully around and turning the dorsal **Z**, the right club first swings in to the left, and then out to a horizontal position on the right; and while the left, descending the arc D, swings in to a horizontal position, and then out to a horizontal position also, the right moving to the left ascends the arc and sweeping gracefully around turns the dorsal. Thus all the movements of No. **3,** are exactly reversed. Vary the movement by throwing in occasionally the double front circle A ·resuming afterwards the regular motion. The volume of the swing may be increased by turning the dorsal three times, adding a corresponding number of arc sweeps.

6.

Z   arc D   arc C   (S)   1.

Starting from the first goal and moving towards each other, both clubs rise on the arc, sweep gracefully around to the right and left and turn at the same moment the upper dorsal **Z**: then descending the arc D, they pass in front to a horizontal position, the arms being crossed upon the breast, and back again to the other horizontal position, the arms being extended at length on opposite sides of the person. From this position the swing is repeated. When performed with spirit it affords vigorous exercise, stretching out the arms and expanding the chest finely.

7.

Arc E and the circlet m in transit.   (S)   1.
Return.   Arc G and the circlet l in transit.   (S)   7.

In this swing the clubs move on the side arcs, in parallel sweeps which cross the front arcs at right angles. From the first goal

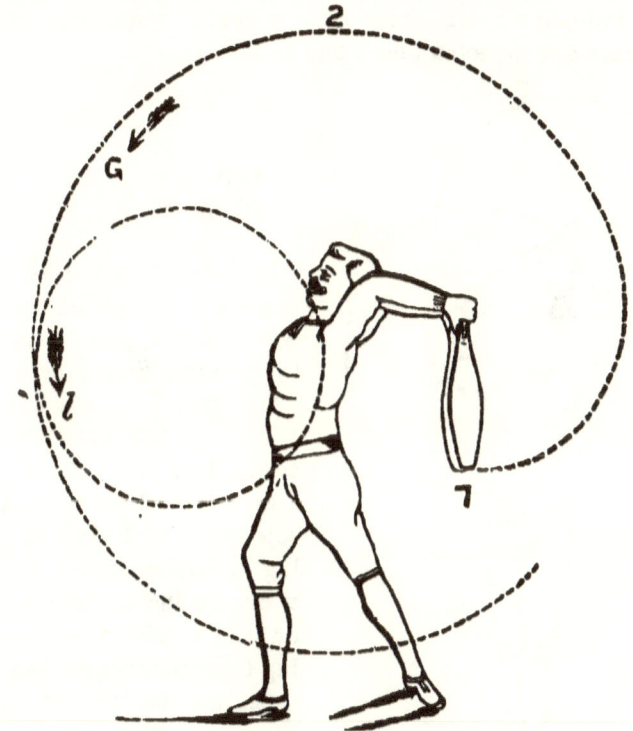

Fig. 45.

swing both clubs directly forwards on the side arcs E. As they are passing the breast, whirl the m circlets, allowing the clubs to

6*

drop back over the shoulders.   On the return sweep, denoted by
G, whirl the 1 circlets as they pass the breast, and let them con-
tinue on, passing beyond the goals as far as the arms will permit,
the body retaining its erect position.   Vary the swing by sometimes turning two circlets on the ascent and two on the descent.
(Eng. 45.)

Another variation consists in starting the clubs from opposite
points; for instance, the left club from goal 1 and the right from
goal 7, each turning a circlet, sometimes two circlets, as it ascends and descends.   Observe that in this swing the circlets nei-
ther precede nor follow the long sweep, but are introduced in
transit.

8.

The following exercises in circlets, having some points of resemblance are collected under one head:

Fig. 37.

1st.

$$\left. \begin{array}{l} \text{Left club} \quad 1 \quad n \\ \text{Right} \quad \text{''} \quad n \quad 1 \end{array} \right\} \text{(T)} \quad 3.$$

In this exercise the clubs turn
constantly in parallel circles,
which is the essential point of
the swing.   Swing both clubs
up to goal 3 on the left side.
With the left club turn the
circlet 1 on the outside of the
arm, followed by n on the inside, while with the right, moving in parallel curves, you turn
n on the inside followed by 1
on the outside.   After whirling these parallel circlets a few
times on the left side, swing
across on the front arc and
repeat them on the right.
(Eng. 37.)

2d.

Left club m o}(T) 3.
Right "   o m}

From the same point on the left side, reversing the parallel circlets, whirl m on the outside and o on the inside of the left arm; also o on the inside and m on the outside of the right arm. Swing across and repeat on the right side.

3d.

Duplex r and s (T) 6.

Swing the clubs up to a horizontal position on the left side at the height of the shoulders, holding them parallel at arm's length.

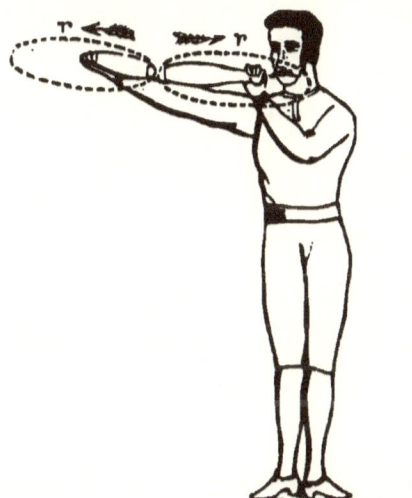

Turn with both clubs the horizontal circlet r, emphasizing the parallelism. Swing across on the front arc and repeat. Also reverse the movement, turning the outward horizontal circlet s with both clubs, traversing the arc as before. (Eng. 43.)

4th.

Left club l }
Right "   m } Continuous. 4.

Holding both clubs vertically in front at goal 4, twirl them in opposite directions, dropping the left forwards and the right backwards and vice versa. Also start one club in advance of the other, each turning the forward circlet l, the second following the first at an interval of half a revolution, producing a similar effect. Keep both clubs twirling without any suspension of motion. The ability to twirl these circlets swiftly comes from persistent drilling. Smoothness and uniformity of motion are more to be desired than great speed.

Fig. 43.

5th.

$$\text{Return.} \quad \left.\begin{array}{cc} 1 & n \\ o & m \end{array}\right\}\text{(S)} \quad 4.$$

Holding the clubs vertically in front of the breast at goal **4**, whirl quickly the circlet l followed by n, lodging the clubs under the arms. In this case n can be only partially turned. Reverse the movement, turning o followed by m, dropping the clubs over the shoulders, the o being only partially turned.

The armpit position of the clubs is occasionally assumed by the swinger for a moment's rest. Other positions of rest are, clubs pendent at the sides (goal **1**), vertical in front (goal **4**), and depending from the shoulders, (goal **7**). (Eng. 42).

Fig. 42.

6th.

$$\left.\begin{array}{l}\text{Left club horizontal and rigid.} \\ \text{Right " arc } C \ \mathbf{Y} \ \mathbf{2} \ \text{arc } C \ 1.\end{array}\right\}\text{(T)} \quad 6.$$

Swing both clubs up to a horizontal position on the left side, which is a point of departure denoted by **6**. Hold the left club at this point stubbornly, with straight arm and stiff elbow, while the right club traversing the front arc turns the upper dorsal **Y**, then makes an arm's length sweep on each side of the extended left arm, turning finally the circlet 1. Both clubs then are swung across to the corresponding point on the right side, where the right arm and club are stubbornly held in a horizontal position while the left executes the foregoing movements. Heighten the effect by adding occasionally to the other motions the horizontal circlet r turned either above or below the rigid arm.

7th.

Left club rigid **3.**
Right " **Y** C or **Z** D **2.**

This exercise also consists in holding one club stationary at arm's length, while the other executes some formula which may be selected for the moment. For example, swing the left club up to goal **3,** holding it rigid and motionless while the right club performs several times in succession the formula **Y** C: then extend the right club, holding it motionless at goal **3** on the right side. while the left executes the same formula. Practice the formula **Z** D in the same way.

9.

The following swings being composed of arcs only are treated under a single head:

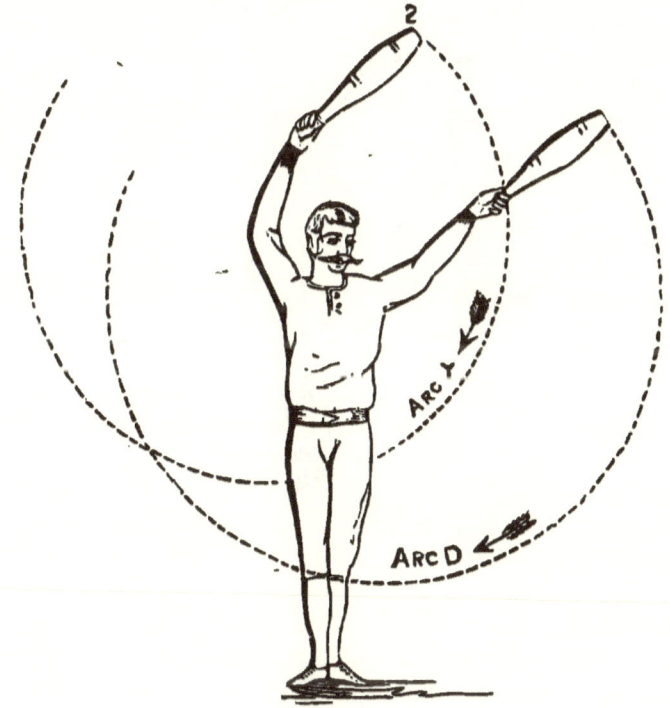

Fig. 38.

1st.

Arc Y   arc D   (F)   3.

Swing the left club up to goal 3 on the left side, the right club taking a position about eighteen inches above it in the same vertical plane, parallel to it and pointing in the same direction. Bring the right club by the dorsal arc Y to goal 3 on the right side, while the left traversing the front arc D comes to a position about eighteen inches above it in the same vertical plane, parallel to it and pointing in the same direction. Repeat the movement from the right side, the left club returning by the dorsal arc and the right by the front arc. As the clubs come to

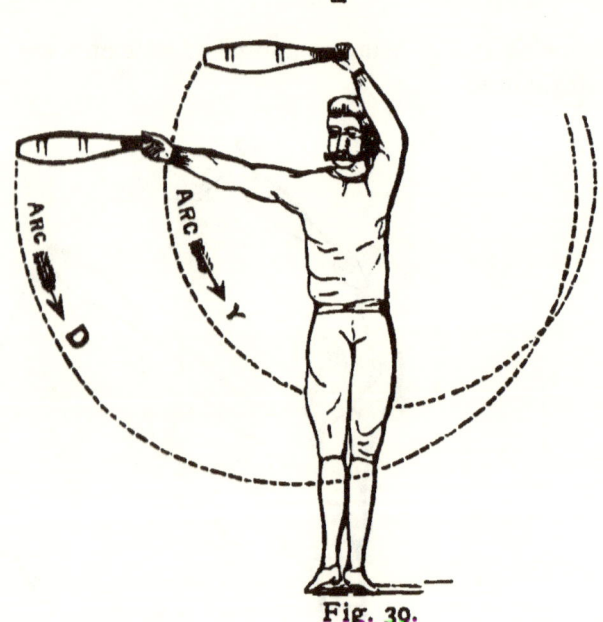

Fig. 39.

position on either side, thrust the arms out with vigor, to give emphasis to the parallelism, which is the prominent feature of the swing. (Eng. 38.)

Practice the same movement from goal 6, the clubs being held at the start in a horizontal position, instead of at an angle of forty-five degrees. In this case, the sweep of the arc is a half circle instead of a three-quarter. (Eng. 39.)

2d.

Arc Z   arc C   (F)   3.

Swing the left club up to goal **3** on the left side, the right taking a parallel position as in the previous swing.   Drop the right club in front, bringing it by the arc C to goal **3** on the right side. The left club, by the arc Z comes to position eighteen inches above it, parallel to it, and pointing in the same direction.   In the return movement, the left club takes the front arc, and the right the dorsal.   Impart emphasis to the parallelism by thrusting the arms out briskly.

Practice this movement also from goal **6**, the clubs taking a horizontal position and sweeping only a semi-circle.

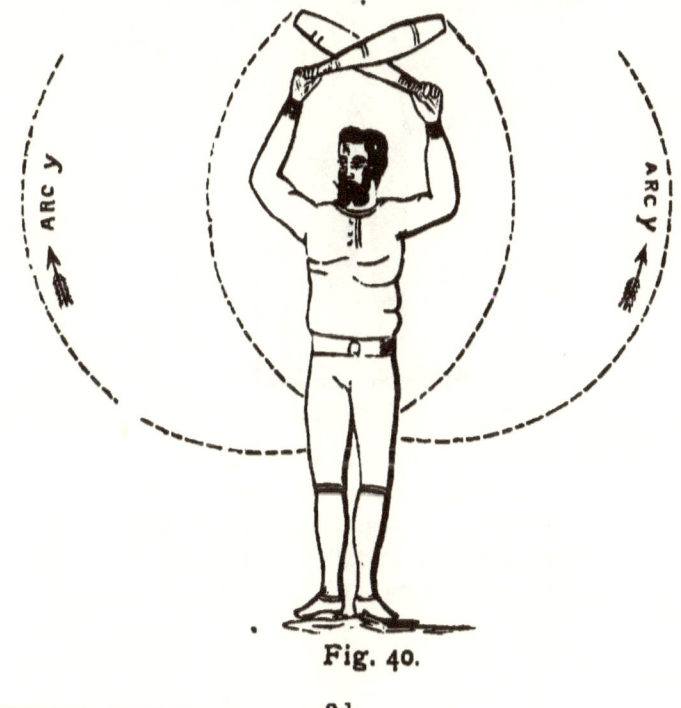

Fig. 40.

3d.

Arc D   arc Y   (S)   3.

Throw the left club up to goal **3** on the left side, and the right to goal **3** on the right side.   With both clubs sweep the front arc, bringing them to a position above the head, crossed like the letter **X**. From this position return by the dorsal **Y** to the points of departure. (Eng. 40.)

Practice this movement from goal **6,** the clubs being held at the start horizontally at arm's length on opposite sides of the person. Sweep the front arc with both clubs, bringing them to

Fig. 41.

a horizontal position directly over the head, one above the other, parallel and pointing in opposite directions. Return by the dorsal arcs **Y** to the points of departure. In all these movements the front arc is somewhat curtailed in order to bring the clubs directly over the head. (Eng. 41.)

4th.

Arc **Z** arc **C** (S) **3.**

Swing the clubs up to goal **3** on opposite sides. From these points both clubs traverse the dorsal arcs **Z,** coming to a position above the head crossed like the letter **X**. Drop both clubs in front, returning them by the arc **C** to the starting points.

Practice this swing from goal 6, holding the clubs horizontally at the start, and bringing them by the dorsal arcs to a horizontal position over the head, returning by the front arcs C to the starting points.

5th.

Left club arc D arc Y
Right "   arc Z arc C (F) 6.

Swing the left club up to goal 6 on the left side and the right to the same goal on the right side. With the left club describe the front arc D and at the same time with the right club, the dorsal arc Z, thus bringing the clubs directly over the head, in a horizontal position, one above the other, parallel, and pointing in opposite directions. Then return the left club to its original position by the dorsal arc Y, while the right returns by the front arc C. Presently, change the exercise by practicing the first part of the formula with the right club, and the second part with the left.

6.

The following exercises on dorsal arcs may be taken in the review:

1st.

Left club dorsal arc D
Right "   "   " C (T) 6.

Point both clubs to the sixth goal on the left side, holding the right club behind the person and parallel to the left. Swing both clubs to and fro behind the person.

2d.

Left club 1 dorsal arc D
Right " .   "   " C (T) 6.

Connect the circlet 1 with the dorsal arc movement. First, (the clubs pointing as in the previous exercise,) turn the circlet with the left, swinging both to the opposite goal; then turn the circlet with the right club, both swinging back to the original position.

7

3d.

Left club m   dorsal arc $\left.\begin{array}{c} D \\ C \end{array}\right\}$ (T) 6.
Right "   "   "

This exercise is like the preceding, except that the backward circlet m takes the place of the forward circlet l. These several exercises may be executed simultaneously as well as alternately.

NOTE.—Nearly all the elementary circles and arcs used in this book have now been illustrated in the engravings. The swings described in the following chapter will be expressed by the formulas only, this being the most intelligible and satisfactory method of representing swings which involve more than two movements.

CHAPTER III.

SECTION 1.

THOSE COMPRISING THREE OR MORE CIRCLES.

1.

Every one at all conversant with Indian club swinging must have observed the marked and peculiar tendency of the hands to make the same movement. The following eight examples have been selected with special reference to overcoming this inclination and disciplining each hand to move independently of the other.

1st.

Left club 1 continuously }
Right " Y G   .   } 2.

From the second point of departure, which is the foot of each club as it is held perpendicularly at arm's length above the head, turn the circlet 1 continuously with the left club, while the right executes and repeats time after time the formula composed of the upper dorsal circle Y, followed by the forward side circle G. As the left club whirls the circlet, let the right describe the first circle of the formula, and as the left repeats the circlet, let the right sweep the second circle of the formula. After a while, execute the formula with the left club while the right turns the circlet continuously.

2d.

Left club Y continuous⎫
Right "   Y C   ⎬2.

Considerable tact is required to perform this example smoothly, from the fact that, at every alternate sweep, the dorsal circle must be turned by both clubs. Practice will soon teach you to make a proper allowance for the crossing of the clubs to avoid contact. The detail of the swing is like the preceding.

3d.

Left club Y continuous⎫
Right "   Z D   ⎬2.

4th.

Left club Z continuous⎫
Right "   Y C   ⎬2.

5th.

Left club Z continuous⎫
Right "   Z D   ⎬2.

6th.

Left club p continuous⎫
Right "   W p   ⎬1.

7th.

Left club r I 5.
Right "   p W 1.

8th.

Left club s J 5.
Right "   q X 1.

The student is recommended to devise other examples for the purpose of training the hands to independent action, which is quite an important attainment in the art of club swinging.

2.

$$\left. \begin{array}{l} \text{Left club } \textbf{2 1} \\ \text{Right } \text{``} \quad \text{G} \end{array} \right\}^{\textbf{2.}}$$

This formula requires two revolutions of the left club to one of the right. From goal **2** start both clubs at the same moment, whirling the circlet twice in succession with the left club, while the right describes the straight arm side circle G. After a while, describe the large circle with the left club and the two circlets with the right. Practice also the following formulas or devise similar ones.

$$\left. \begin{array}{l} \text{Left club } \textbf{2 Y} \\ \text{Right } \text{``} \quad \text{C or D} \end{array} \right\}^{\textbf{2.}}$$

$$\left. \begin{array}{l} \text{Left club } \textbf{2 Z} \\ \text{Right } \text{``} \quad \text{D or C} \end{array} \right\}^{\textbf{2.}}$$

$$\left. \begin{array}{l} \text{Left club } \textbf{2 Y} \\ \text{Right } \text{``} \quad \text{G} \end{array} \right\}^{\textbf{2.}}$$

3.

$$\left. \begin{array}{l} \text{Left club } \textbf{Y C} \\ \text{Right } \text{``} \quad \textbf{Z D} \end{array} \right\}^{(T)} \ \textbf{2.}$$

Swing both clubs up to goal **2,** holding them perpendicularly above the head and parallel to each other. From this point both clubs move at the same moment, in concert throughout, with uniform speed and in parallel circles. Starting to the right, drop both over the right shoulder, the left club describing the dorsal Y followed by the front circle C, and the right the dorsal Z followed by the front circle D. These movements constitute the first division of the swing. After repeating this concert movement four or five times on the right side, bring the clubs squarely to the front, stopping at the goals. Now execute the second division by dropping both clubs over the left shoulder, the right club describing the dorsal Y followed by the front circle C, and the left the dorsal Z followed by D. This swing illustrates the union of the divisions by the third method, which consists in executing a formula a specified number of times on one side of

7*

the person, and then repeating it the same number of times on the other side.

The above swing is often rendered more ornamental by introducing the 1 circlets between the back and front circles, just at the moment when the clubs emerge from behind the shoulders. The formula then becomes

$$\left.\begin{array}{l} \text{Left club } \mathbf{Y} \quad 1 \quad \text{C} \\ \text{Right `` } \quad \mathbf{Z} \quad 1 \quad \text{D} \end{array}\right\}\text{(T)} \quad \mathbf{2.}$$

Instead of bringing the clubs squarely to the front, the transfer of the swing from one side to the other is more frequently effected by quickly reversing the movement of the clubs as they reach the upper dorsal circles. For instance, if you are executing the swing on the right side and wish to change to the left, the moment you reach the dorsal circles, extend the right arm longitudinally to the left, passing the right club over the left shoulder and head, causing it to sweep the circle C in front instead of D, while the left moving in concert is made to sweep the front circle D instead of C. A somewhat peculiar swing is produced by changing the direction of the sweep at every revolution of the clubs in front, the formula in this case being

$$\left.\begin{array}{l} \text{Left club } \mathbf{Y} \quad \text{D} \\ \text{Right `` } \quad \mathbf{Z} \quad \text{C} \end{array}\right\}\text{(T)} \quad \mathbf{2.}$$

By simply changing the expression of the third formula two other swings may be produced, composed of the same circles but following each other in a different order of succession thus:

$$\left.\begin{array}{l} \text{Left club } \mathbf{Y} \quad \text{C} \\ \text{Right `` } \quad \text{D} \quad \mathbf{z} \end{array}\right\}\text{(T)} \quad \mathbf{2.}$$

$$\left.\begin{array}{l} \text{Left club } \mathbf{z} \quad \text{D} \\ \text{Right `` } \quad \text{C} \quad \mathbf{Y} \end{array}\right\}\text{(T)} \quad \mathbf{2.}$$

4.

$$\left.\begin{array}{l} \text{Left club } \text{C} \quad \mathbf{Y} \\ \text{Right `` } \quad \text{D} \quad \mathbf{z} \end{array}\right\}\text{(T)} \quad \mathbf{2.} \quad \tfrac{1}{2}\text{ circle interval.}$$

In starting this swing let the right club follow the left at an interval of half a circle. Swing the clubs up to goal 2. Start

the left club to the right on the front circle C and when it
reaches the feet, start the right club in the same direction on
the front circle D. With the left club, as it ascends the arc on
the left, turn the dorsal Y and a moment later, with the right
club, turn the dorsal Z, both passing again into the front circles,
the right following the left at the fixed interval before named.
After several revolutions, shift the movement to the left side,
either by bringing the clubs to the front, or by the quick transfer movement previously explained. This swing may be varied
by making two dorsal turns to one in front. The start is often
taken from the first goal.

5.

$$\text{Left club} \quad \begin{matrix} A & W \\ B & X \end{matrix} \Big\} (T) \quad \textbf{1.}$$
Right "

This is a concert swing, similar to No. 3, only involving the
lower series of back and front circles instead of the upper. The
lower series is equally as interesting and important as the upper,
and the skilful performer should be able to turn its circles with
equal facility. From the first goal sweep the front circles simultaneously with both clubs moving to the right, the left tracing
A and the right B. As the clubs descend the arc on the left
side they separate momentarily, the left passing behind the person and turning the lower dorsal W, while the right, with the
momentum gathered in the descent, is made to turn the other
lower dorsal X by bringing the right hand quickly under the
armpit and behind the hip, as previously explained. After several repetitions, reverse the movement by starting both clubs to
the left. When the above swing has been thoroughly learned in
the form given, it may be embellished by adding the front circlets p and q after the back circles W and X. The formula will
then read,

$$\text{Left club} \quad \begin{matrix} A & W & p \\ B & X & q \end{matrix} \Big\} (T) \quad \textbf{1.}$$
Right "

6.

Left club A W $\Big\}$(T) 1. ¼ circle interval.
Right " B X

Start the left club to the right and when it reaches a point directly over the head, follow with the right moving in the same direction. After several revolutions in this direction, reverse the movement by starting the clubs to the left. When thoroughly acquired, add the circlets p and q as in the previous swing.

7.

Left club Y X $\Big\}$(T) 1.
Right " Z W

This concert swing is composed of the four dorsal circles. From point 1 sweep both clubs up the arc on the left side, turning the upper dorsal Y with the left club, and Z with the right, after which, as they descend on the right side turn the lower dorsal X with the left club, and W with the right, both clubs re-appearing at point 1 to repeat. After repeating several times, start the clubs up the arc on the right side, the right club turning Y and the left Z in the ascent, and the right X and the left W in the descent. When the swing has become familiar in its plain form, introduce the 1 circlets after the upper dorsals Y and Z, and the circlets p and q after the lower dorsals W and X. The formula then becomes,

Left club Y ∣ X q $\Big\}$(T) 1.
Right " Z ∣ W p

8.

A W Z (F) 1.

Grouping. AW, WZ, ZA.

When the left club describes A the right describes W ; when the left turns W the right turns Z ; when the left turns Z the right turns A. This coupling of circles is expressed in the grouping. The first division of the swing is the formula exe-

cuted with the left club; the second, with the right club. The
detail of the movements is as follows: The left club moving to
the right from the first goal sweeps the straight-arm circle A,
passing in the same sweep behind the person and turning the
lower dorsal circle W ; then coming to the front it ascends
directly in front of the face, and bearing well round to the left
turns the upper dorsal Z. Meantime the right club, commencing
with the second movement of the formula turns first the dorsal
W, then ascending directly in front of the face and bearing well
round to the right, turns the upper dorsal Z, then descending,
sweeps finally the straight-arm circle A. This is a noble swing,
inducing a free and unembarrassed manipulation, suggestive of
a perfect mastery of the art.

> " It was not framed for village churls,
>   But for high dames and mighty earls."

9.   .

A W Z (S) 1.

With both clubs describe the circle A, followed by W, in one
continuous sweep, the clubs crossing in front of and also behind
the person. As they ascend in front of the face, sweep them
well around to the right and left with graceful curvature, turning finally the upper dorsal Z, after which they descend again
into the front circle to repeat.

10.

B X Y (F) 1.

Grouping. BX, XY, YB.

The first motion of the right club may be *feinted*, there being
no accumulated force to assist in turning it. In consequence of
the clubs passing into the circle B at a point over the head after
turning the upper dorsal Y, and again leaving it to turn the
lower, it becomes really an arc instead of a complete circle, after
the first sweep of the left club. This abbreviation or clipping
of the circles is sometimes unavoidable in meeting the exigencies
of particular swings. It will be noticed also that at the above

point the circles B and C coincide. The rule is to adhere strictly to the formula, using the specific name of the circle there given, the coalescence of the different contours giving rise to no practical difficulty in its execution.

This swing is often executed from the second point of departure, in which case the lower dorsal X follows a descending sweep on each side, which is an advantage in starting the swing. When executed from this point the formula becomes

Y   C   X (F) 2.

Grouping. YC, CX, XY.

In this case the circle C is clipped. If we regard the arc C merely as a connecting link between the upper and lower dorsals, the swing may be reduced to two movements, as in No. 33, Chap. II, Sec. 1.

11.

B X Y (S) 1.

Execute the circles successively with both clubs. When started from goal 2 the formula is Y C X (S) 2.

Practice also the reverse formulas to this.

Z D W (F) 2.

Z D W (S) 2.

12.

q C 2 Y (F) 4. 2.

Grouping. qY, CY.

In this swing the left club starts from the fourth goal and the right from the second. Swing both clubs up to goal 4. From this position raise the right perpendicularly to goal 2. Facing to the right, turn the circlet q with the left club. When turned at this position q virtually coincides with 1, inasmuch as the club drops forward and comes up on the outside of the arm. At the same moment turn the dorsal Y with the right club. As soon as q is turned with the left club, extend the arm at length in the same vertical plane, and describe the complete front circle C, the right club, at the same moment turning the dorsal Y a second time. Now face to the left and repeat, turning the circlet q in front with the right club while the left turns the dorsal Y, and the large circle C with the right while the left repeats the dorsal.

A dramatic air may be imparted to this swing by assuming the sparring attitude as you turn the circlet, bending the knees and setting back the body on the hips; then rise and throw the club to the utmost height as you sweep the large circle. In this way considerable exercise is obtained for the lower limbs by constantly turning from side to side, sinking and rising as you alternate from the small to the large circle. If the performer chooses he may execute this swing a definite number of times consecutively on each side, uniting the divisions by the third method.

13.

q C 2 Y (S) 4.

In this form of the swing the body is kept square to the front.

14.

p D 2 Z (F) 3.

Grouping. pZ, DZ.

Extend the clubs to goal 3 on opposite sides. Whirl the circlet p with the left club, relaxing the grasp and holding on to the club with the thumb and fingers, and at the same time turn the dorsal Z with the right club. Then with the left sweep the great circle D, repeating the dorsal with the right. Now change the movement by turning the dorsal twice in succession with the left club while the right executes the circlet, followed by the circle. Keep the feet in position, only swaying the body as the clubs change from one side to the other.

15.

p D 2 Z (S) 3.

Describe each circle successively with both clubs; swing them well out to the right and left with graceful curvature previous to turning the double dorsal.

The student should now begin to exercise his inventive powers in devising original swings. Any circles or arcs which glide smoothly into each other may be wrought into swings. He will soon find a peculiar fascination in devising swings for his own practice and also take an unwonted interest in executing those which are the product of his own ingenuity.

16.

Y C q (F) 2.

Grouping. YC, Cq, qY.

The circlet is turned in front at the first goal, the circle C being clipped. In turning the circlet, seek to impart sufficient impulse to the club to send it briskly up the ascending arc. This impulse assists materially in turning the dorsal Y.

17.

Y C q (S) 2.

When you turn the circlet with both clubs, send them well out to the right and left, sweeping up the ascending arcs with fully extended arms. The quality of the swing depends largely on the impulsion given to the circlets.

18.

Z D p (F) 3.

Grouping. ZD, Dp, pZ.

The circlet p is turned at goal 3 in front of the extended arm. Practice the divisions well before making the union, as the order in which the circles follow each other is somewhat novel. In sweeping the large front circle, be careful to carry the club well out on the side previous to turning the circlet. The more perfectly the circles are made, the more exhilarating the exercise becomes.

19.

Z D p (S) 3.

The start may be taken from the second goal if preferred.

20.

A W p (F) 1.

Grouping. AW, Wp, pA.

21.

A W p (S) 1.

In this swing as well as in the preceding the first two circles are made in an unbroken sweep.

22.

B X q (F) 1.

Grouping. BX, Xq, qB.

23.

B X q (S) 1.

24.

Y C q B (F) 2.

Grouping. YC, Cq, qB, BY.

In this swing C is clipped, while B is overswept the distance from q to Y. The union is by the first method, the left club tracing each circle in succession and the right also tracing each successively, beginning with the second.

For the reason already assigned, namely, to discipline, strengthen and develop the left arm, which is usually neglected, in stating the formulas and in describing the swings, precedence has been conceded to the left club. The student, however, should accustom himself to perform the swings either hand foremost with equal facility. Execute the above swing, the right hand taking the lead.

8

25.

Y C q B (S) 2.

In this connection practice the following formulas:

Z D p A (F) 2.
Z D p A (S) 2.

Left club n 1)(F) 3.
Right " Y C)   2.

p l W (F) 1. 6.
p l W (S) 1.
q m X (F) 1. 6.
q m X (S) 1.

In the last four examples p and q are turned in front from the first goal, and l and m at arm's length at the side from the sixth goal.

26.

A p W Z (F) 1. 3.

Grouping. Ap, pW, WZ, ZA.

The circlet p is whirled at arm's length at the side. Extend the arms to goal 3 on each side of the person. The left club first sweeps a complete straight-arm circle in front. As the club comes around to the goal again it whirls, as high up as possible, the circlet p; then it passes behind the hips where it turns the lower dorsal W; after which, coming quickly to the front and ascending, it describes finally the upper dorsal Z, which completes the first section of the swing, the same series of circles traced with the right club forming the second section. The union is by the first method, the left club describing A as the right whirls p; the left whirling p as the right turns W; the left W as the right Z; the left Z as the right A.

This is a very graceful swing when practice has rendered the movements easy and familiar; and I can conceive of no exercise better calculated to secure perfect freedom in the use of the arms or a finer development, than this with the Indian clubs. It is alike adapted to ladies and gentlemen and undoubtedly should form a part of the daily curriculum of schools and colleges in the department of physical exercise. Solomon affirms of the virtuous woman, "She girdeth her loins with strength, and strengtheneth her arms." Furthermore, the exercise of club swinging is eminently social. What sight more interesting than a company of youths and misses, apparelled in neat and comely uniforms, swinging the Indian clubs, in pairs or coteries of four, five or six, keeping time and following, when convenient, the accompaniment of the piano or other musical instrument? Such a scene calls vividly to mind the poet's holiday picture;

> " How often have I blest the coming day,
> When toil remitting lent its turn to play,
> And all the village train, from labor free,
> Led up their sports beneath the spreading tree,
> While many a pastime circled in the shade,
> The young contending as the old surveyed;
> And many a gambol frolick'd o'er the ground,
> And sleights of hand and feats of strength went round."

27.

A p W Z (S) 1.

Trace each circle with both clubs in the order of the formula.

28.

B q X Y (F) 1.

Grouping. Bq, qX, XY, YB.

29.

B q X Y (S) 1.

This formula may be taken to illustrate the great variety of ways in which the various circles made with the clubs may be combined into swings. By applying the rule of permutations twenty-four variations can be formed from these four circles, all of which are capable of being reduced to practice by a skilful manipulator of the clubs. The formulas are as follows:

B	q	X	Y	q	B	X	Y	X	B	q	Y	Y	B	q	X
B	q	Y	X	q	B	Y	X	X	B	Y	q	Y	B	X	q
B	X	q	Y	q	X	B	Y	X	q	B	Y	Y	q	B	X
B	X	Y	q	q	X	Y	B	X	q	Y	B	Y	q	X	B
B	Y	q	X	q	Y	B	X	X	Y	B	q	Y	X	B	q
B	Y	X	q	q	Y	X	B	X	Y	q	B	Y	X	q	B

30.

A W p Z (F) 1.

Grouping. AW, Wp, pZ, ZA.

This formula, like the preceding, is susceptible of twenty-four variations, some of which, of course, are executed with greater facility than others. The above form is one of the best as the circles succeed each other in an easy and natural way, with full and generous sweeps. Unite the divisions also by the second and third methods according to the following formulas:

$$A \quad W \quad p \quad Z \quad (S) \quad 1.$$

Left club $A \quad W \quad p \quad Z$ }(T) 1.
Right " $B \quad X \quad q \quad Y$

Such swings as these, which require vigorous effort should not be practiced immediately after a full meal. The following rule, expressed in homely rhythm, and broadly stated withal, is easy to remember:

    " Rise early and take exercise in plenty,
    But always take it with your stomach empty."

SECTION 2.

SWINGS COMPRISING THREE OR MORE CIRCLES OR ARCS.

1.

p A arc B W (F) 1.

Grouping. p arc B, AW.

With the left club whirl impulsively the circlet p followed by the large circle A, and at the same moment swing the right club out horizontally to the right and then in behind the person, turn-ing the dorsal **W**. Next whirl the circlet impulsively with the right club followed by the front circle, while the left swings out horizontally to goal **6** and in behind the person, turning the dor-sal. The sleight of turning the circlet with one club while the other shoots out horizontally is soon acquired.

2.

p A arc B W (8) 1.

With both clubs first whirl the circlet, then sweep the front circle allowing the clubs to cross in front as they come in; then send both out to a horizontal position at arm's length on opposite sides, from which points they pass in behind the person, execut-ing the double dorsal.

3.

Left club Z Z arc D arc C arc D $\Big\}$(T) 3.
Right " arc C Y arc C arc Z arc C

Start both clubs simultaneously from goal **3**, on the left side. The left club turns the dorsal **Z** twice while the right traverses the front arc and turns the dorsal **Y** once; both clubs now cross the front arc in company to the third goal on the right; separat-ing at this point the left swings back on the front arc to goal **8** on the left, while the right club reaches the same point by the dorsal arc **Z**; then both recross in concert to goal **3** on the right. The swing is quite easy, consisting mostly of swinging the clubs to and fro on the front arcs. We have given only the first divis-ion, the second being the same movements repeated from the third goal on the right side.

4.

Left club Y arc C $\Big\}$(T) 2.
Right " arc D Z 6.

This swing is peculiar inasmuch as each club immediately re-traces its own movement. Start the left club from the second goal and the right club from the sixth goal, on the right side, which is the arm's length horizontal position. The left club

8*

turns the dorsal **Y** and sweeps the front arc C to goal **6** on the left; the right sweeps the front arc D and turns the dorsal **Z**. In the second division the right retraces its previous movement by turning the dorsal **Y** and sweeping the front arc C to the sixth goal on the right, while the left also retraces by swinging back on the arc D and turning the dorsal **Z**. This swing affords a fine stretch for the arms as the clubs swing out and stop at the sixth goal on either side.

5.

$$\left. \begin{array}{l} \text{Left club } \mathbf{Z} \quad \text{arc } D \\ \text{Right } `` \quad \text{arc } C \quad \mathbf{Y} \end{array} \right\} (\text{T}) \quad \mathbf{3.}$$

Both clubs start from goal **3** on the left side. First division: the left club turns the dorsal **Z** and sweeps the front arc D as far as goal **3** on the right, while the right club traverses the front arc C and turns the dorsal **Y**. Second division: the right club turns the dorsal **Z** and sweeps the front arc D to goal **3** on the left, while the left club traverses the front arc C and turns the dorsal **Y**.

6.

$$\left. \begin{array}{l} \text{Left club } \quad \mathbf{Z} \;\; \mathbf{Z} \;\; D \;\; \mathbf{Z} \;\; D \;\; \mathbf{Z} \;\; \text{arc } D \\ \text{Right } `` \quad \text{arc } C \;\; \mathbf{Y} \;\; C \;\; \mathbf{Y} \;\; \mathbf{Y} \;\; \mathbf{Y} \;\; \text{arc } C \end{array} \right\} (\text{T}) \quad \mathbf{3.}$$

The clubs move simultaneously from the third goal on the left side, the left turning the dorsal **Z**, the right swinging across on the front arc C; the left turning the second dorsal **Z**, the right turning the first **Y**; both now sweeping together the front circle which is D for the left club and C for the right; the left club turning the third **Z**, the right the second **Y**; the left now sweeping alone the front circle D, the right turning the third ·**Y**; lastly, in concert, the left turning the fourth **Z**, the right the fourth **Y** and swinging across on the front arc to goal **3** on the right side. The swing is less difficult than the formula would indicate, as the clubs for the most part move in concert, executing parallel circles, while the reckoning is easily kept by counting the dorsal turns of either club, of which there are four.

7.

Y arc C W arc B (F) 2. 6.

Grouping. YW, arc C arc B.

The left club starting from the second goal turns Y and sweeps the front arc C to goal 6 on the left. At the same moment the right club, starting from goal 6 on the right, and, swinging behind the person, turns -W and ascends arc B on the right. The left club, starting anew, as it were, from the sixth goal on the left, turns W and ascends the arc B, while the right club, turning Y sweeps the front arc to goal 6 on the right, its first point of departure. The movement is somewhat chary and elusive, and on that account more captivating. The divisions of this swing may be united in each of the three methods, affording a fine illustration of the three forms of union applied to a single formula. The ingenious student will be able to apply the third form to a number of the swings described in this book where only the first and second methods are exhibited in the text. A critical review of the swings with this object in view will afford entertainment as well as exercise.

Practice the second and third forms of this swing and also the reverse, as indicated in the following formulas:

Y arc C W arc B (S) 2.
Y arc C W arc B (T) 2.
Z arc D X arc A (F) 2.
Z arc D X arc A (S) 2.
Z arc D X arc A (T) 2.

8.

Left club   W p p arc C ⎱ (F) 6.
Right " arc D p p arc C ⎰

Extend the clubs to goal 6, on opposite sides, pointing outwards. Sweep the back circle W with the left club, followed by the circlet p in front; at the same time swing in the right club on the short arc D also turning the circlet p in front. Repeat the circlet with both clubs, allowing them to cross in front, after which both swing out on the arc C to the original position.

Then the right club sweeps the back circle **W** while the left takes the arc **D**, and so on alternately. Try the following formulas:

$$\begin{array}{llllll}
 & \mathbf{W} & p & p & \text{arc } \mathbf{C} & \text{(S)} & \mathbf{6.} \\
 & \mathbf{W} & p & p & \text{arc } \mathbf{C} & \text{(T)} & \mathbf{6.} \\
\text{Left club} & \mathbf{X} & q & q & \text{arc } \mathbf{D} & \\
\text{Right ``} & \text{arc } \mathbf{C} & q & q & \text{arc } \mathbf{D} & \\
 & \mathbf{X} & q & q & \text{arc } \mathbf{D} & \text{(S)} & \mathbf{6.} \\
 & \mathbf{X} & q & q & \text{arc } \mathbf{D} & \text{(T)} & \mathbf{6.}
\end{array}$$

Left club · **X** q q arc **D** } (F) **6.**
Right " arc **C** q q arc **D**

9.

Left club m **Y** } (F) **6.**
Right " 1 arc **C**

Extending both clubs to goal **6** on the left side, whirl the circlet m with the left club, and 1 with the right; then the dorsal **Y** with the left, while the right swings across to goal **6** on the right side. From this point the right club turns m and **Y**, while the left turns 1 and sweeps the arc. The union by (S) and (T) may be applied to this formula and also to the reverse.

Left club 1 arc **D** } (F) **6.**
Right " m **Z**

———————

Without extending further the list of detached swings, the following chapter will be occupied in presenting in new and in teresting relations some of those already described.

" To please the fancy is no trifling good,
  Where health is studied; for whatever moves
  The mind with calm delight promotes the just
  And natural movements of the harmonious frame."

CHAPTER IV.

SECTION 1.

BIFOLD SWINGS.

Many of the formulas enunciated in the preceding chapters may be rendered at once more interesting and more useful by bifolding or repeating each circle in each division as the swing proceeds. The increased volume of the duplicated swing affords a greater amount of exercise and an agreeable diversity of movement, while at the same time, the distinctive character of each swing is fully retained. The following formulas will serve to illustrate the beauty and practicability of the bifold principle which the student is earnestly recommended to apply to the utmost extent of his ingenuity.

1.

2 | 2 G (F) 2.   Page 35.

From the second goal, whirl the circlet twice with the left club, while with the right, for each turn of the circlet, you sweep the forward side circle. Then whirl two circlets with the right club and two side circles with the left. Swing deliberately, counting the movements, and swaying the body to the right and left as the straight-arm circle changes from side to side. The primitive of each bifold swing will be found on the page given in the formula.

2.

2 | 2 Y (F) 2.   Page 49.

3.

2 1 2 Y (S) 2.   Page 50.

4.

2 Y 2 G (F) 2.   Page 44.

5.

2 q 2 C 4 Y (F) 4. 2.   Page 82.
Grouping. 2 q 2 Y, 2 C 2 Y.

Facing to the right turn the circlet twice at the fourth goal in
front of the breast with the left club, and the dorsal twice with
the right, then the front circle C twice with the left, and two
additional dorsals with the right. Repeat, facing to the left.

6.

2 q 2 C 4 Y (S) 4.   Page 83.

7.

2 Y 2 C 2 q (F) 2.   Page 84.
Grouping. 2 Y 2 C, 2 C 2 q, 2 q 2 Y.

8.

2 Y 2 C 2 q (S) 2.   Page 84.

9.

2 A 2 W (F) 1.   Page 47.

10.

2 A 2 W (S) 1.   Page 47.

11.

2 Y 2 C 2 q 2 B (F) 2.   Page 85.
Grouping. 2 Y 2 C, 2 C 2 q, 2 q 2 B, 2 B 2 Y.

12.

2 Y 2 C 2 q 2 B (S) 2. Page 86.

13.

2 Y 2 C 2 X (F) 2. Page 82.
Grouping. 2 Y 2 C, 2 C 2 X, 2 X 2 Y.

14.

2 Y 2 C 2 X (S) 2. Page 82.

The difficulty of repeating the lower dorsal circles may be obviated by substituting p for W and q for X in the second revolution of the clubs.

15.

2 p 2 D 4 Z (F) 3. Page 83.
Grouping. 2 p 2 Z, 2 D 2 Z.

16.

2 p 2 D 4 Z (S) 3. Page 83.

In the last two formulas, the circlet is turned at goal 3 at arm's length at the side. I think every unprejudiced person must admit that no exercise can be devised better adapted to increase the lung capacity than these bifold swings, notwithstanding the covetous banker's humorous commendation of dumb bells, who, on being teased for money by his daughter, whose name was Belle, replied,

> " Dear Belle, to gain money, sure, silence is best,
> For *dumb* Bells are fittest to open the chest."

SECTION 2.

COMPOUND SWINGS.

Two swings whose movements flow smoothly together may often be united and repeated as one. Frequently a formula and its reverse may be thus joined forming an attractive compound, as in the following examples:

1.

(Y arc C arc D) (Z arc D arc C) (F) **1.**

The component formulas will be found on pages 63 and 64. Execute them successively, passing promptly from the first to the second, repeating the two precisely as one swing. They will soon run smoothly together, forming a new and agreeable combination.

2. (Y arc C arc D) (Z arc D arc C) (S) **1.**
3. (q C 2 Y) (p D 2 Z) (F) **4. 2.** Page 82-3.
4. (q C 2 Y) (p D 2 Z) (S) **4.**
5. (Y C q) (Z D p) (F) **2.** Page 84.
6. (Y C q) (Z D p) (S) **2.**
7. (Y C q B) (Z D p A) (F) **2.** Page 85-6.
8. (Y C q B) (Z D p A) (S) **2.**

Sometimes compounds are formed by uniting a swing which contains the upper series of motions to another which contains the lower series, as in the following examples, in each of which you first execute on both sides the first formula, containing the upper series, and then pass to the second containing the lower series, repeating the two continuously as one swing.

1. (Y arc C arc D) (W p p arc C) (F) **2.**
2. (Y arc C arc D) (W p p arc C) (S) **2.**
3. (Z arc D arc C) (X q q arc D) (F) **2.**
4. (Z arc D arc C) (X q q arc D) (S) **2.**

Compound swings may be bifolded with most pleasing effect as in the following examples:

1. (2 Y 2 C) (2 Z 2 D) (F) **2.** Page 40-2.
2. (2 Y 2 C) (2 Z 2 D) (S) **2.**
3. (Y arc Y D arc D) (Z arc Z C arc C) (F) **2.** Page 70-1.
4. (2 q 2 C 4 Y) (2 p 2 D 4 Z) (F) **4. 2.** Page 82-3.
5. (2 q 2 C 4 Y) (2 p 2 D 4 Z) (S) **4.**
6. (2 Y 2 C 2 q) (2 Z 2 D 2 p) (F) **2.** Page 84.
7. (2 Y 2 C 2 q) (2 Z 2 D 2 p) (S) **2.**
8. (2 Y 2 C 2 q 2 B) (2 Z 2 D 2 p 2 A) (F) **2.** Page 85-6.
9. (2 Y 2 C 2 q 2 B) (2 Z 2 D 2 p 2 A) (S) **2.**

In the third example complete circles are turned on the first circuit, the parallelism taking effect only on the second. In this way many other arc swings may be bifolded.

SECTION 3.

CONTINUOUS SWINGS.

"Strength of heart
And might of limb, but mainly use and skill,
Are winners in this pastime of our king."

Swings in which the transition from one to another is easy and natural may be arranged into lists and executed continuously, presenting an ever varying outline of graceful motions. The student is recommended to construct lists for his own practice, as an opportunity is thus afforded him to weave in his favorite swings, which method, he will find, greatly enhances his interest in the exercise. The following lists are presented more to illustrate the principle of continuity and to invite effort, than to indicate any preference of classification. In continuous swinging each formula of a list may be executed once, or more than once, at the option of the performer. In learning a list, practice the first formula, then the first and second, then the first, second and third, then add the fourth, and so on until the entire list is thoroughly memorized, and the order of arrangement becomes so familiar as to seem perfectly natural and spontaneous.

FIRST LIST.

1. Left club **Y** C $\big\}$(T) 2. Page 77.
   Right " **Z** D

2. Left club C **Y**$\big\}$(T) 2. $\frac{1}{4}$ circle interval. Page 78.
   Right " D **Z**

3. Left club 2 1 arc D $\big\}$(T) 3. Page 62.
   Right " arc C arc D arc C

4. **Y** arc C arc D (F) 1. Page 63.

5. **Z** arc D arc C (F) 1. Page 64.

9

6. Left club 2 Z arc D arc C arc D } (T) 3. Page 89.
   Right " arc C Y arc C arc D arc C }

7. Left club Y arc C } (T) 2. Page 89.
   Right " arc D Z } 6.

8. Left club Z arc D } (T) 3. Page 90.
   Right " arc C Y }

9. Left club o m arc D } (T) 3. Page 61.
   Right " o m arc C }

10. Left club 2 Z D Z D Z arc D } (T) 3. Page 90.
    Right " arc C Y C 3 Y arc C }

❦

SECOND LIST.

1. Y C (F) 2. Page 40.
2. Z D (F) 2. Page 42.
3. Arc Y arc D (F) 3. Page 70.
4. Arc Z arc C (F) 3. Page 71.
5. Y 1 (F) 2. Page 49.
6. Y G (F) 2. Page 44.
7. 1 G (F) 2. Page 35.
8. Left club 3 1 } (F) 2. Page 36.
   Right " 2 1 G }
9. Arc E m in transit (S) 1. }
   Arc G 1 " (S) 7. } Page 65.
10. 1 arc D (T) 6. concert, low and high. Page 61.

THIRD LIST.

1. Parallel circlets 1 n } m o } Page 66–7.
                      n 1 } o m }
2. p A (F) 1. Page 36.
3. q B (F) 1. Page 38.
4. q C 2 Y (F) 4. 2. Page 82.
5. p D 2 Z (F) 3. " 83.
6. Y C q (F) 2. " 84.
7. Z D p (F) 3. " 84.
8. Y C q B (F) 2. " 85.
9. Z D p A (F) 2. " 86.
10. p D (F) 3. " 38.

FOURTH LIST.

1. A   W   Z   (F) 1.   Page 80.
2. B   X   Y   (F) 1.   "   81.
3. A   W   Z   (S) 1.   "   81.
4. B   X   Y   (S) 1.   "   82.
5. q   C   2 Y (S) 4.   "   83.
6. p   D   2 Z (S) 3.   "   83.
7. Y   C   q   (S) 2.   "   84.
8. Z   D   p   (S) 3.   "   84.
9. A   p   W   Z   (F) 1. 3. Page 86.
10. A   p   W   Z   (S) 1.   "   87.

FIFTH LIST.

1. p   X   (F) 1. Page 55.
2. q   X   (F) 1.   "   55.
3. p   W   (F) 1.   "   52.
4. q   W   (F) 1.   "   53.
5. Left club q   X } (T) 1. Concert. Page 56.
    Right "   p   W }
6. Left club n l W } (T) 3. Concert. Page 55.
    Right "   n l X }
7. Left club o m W } (T) 3. Concert. Page 55.
    Right "   o m X }
8. W   Z   (F) 1. Page 50.
9. W   Z   (S) 1.   "   51.
10. Y   X   (F) 2.   "   58.

SIXTH LIST.

1. q   B   W   A   (T) 1. Concert. Page 56.
2. Left club A   W }
    Right "   B   X } (T) 1. Concert. Page 79.
3. Left club A   W }
    Right "   B   X } (T) 1. ½ circle interval. Page 80.
4. Left club Y   X }
    Right "   Z   W } (T) 1. Concert. Page 80.
5. A   W   (F) 1. Page 47.
6. A   W   (S) 1.   "   47.

7.   B   X   (F)   1.   Page 47.
8.   B   X   (S)   1.   "   48.
9.   B   W   (F)   1.   "   48.
10.   B   W   (S)   1.   "   49.

SEVENTH LIST.

1.   2 Y   2 C   (F)   2.   Page 40.
2.   2 Y   2 C   2 X   (F)   2.   "   82.
3.   2 Y   2 C   2 q   (F)   2.   "   84.
4.   2 Y   2 C   2 q   2 B   (F)   2.   "   85.
5.   2 Z   2 D   (F)   2.   "   42.
6.   2 Z   2 D   2 W   (F)   2.   "   82.
7.   2 Z   2 D   2 p   (F)   3.   "   84.
8.   2 Z   2 D   2 p   2 A   (F)   2.   "   86.
9.   2 A   2 W   (S)   1.   "   47.
10.   2 A   2 W   2 Z   (S)   1.   "   81.

EIGHTH LIST.

1.   R   I   (F)   5.   Page 44.
2.   R   I   (S)   5.   "   45.
3.   S   J   (F)   5.   "   46.
4.   S   J   (S)   5.   "   46.
5.   Y   arc C   arc D   (S)   1.   Page 64.
6.   Z   arc D   arc C   (S)   1.   "   64.
7.   p   l   W   (F)   1.   6.   "   86.
8.   p   l   W   (S)   1.   "   86.
9.   q   m   X   (F)   1.   6.   "   86.
10.   p   E   (F)   1.   "   57.

NINTH LIST.

BIFOLD ARC SWINGS.

1.   Left club o   m   o   m   D   arc D } (T)   3.   Page 61.
     Right "   o   m   o   m   C   arc C }
2.   Left club n   l   n   l   arc D   } (T)   3.
     Right "   arc C   arc D   arc C   arc D   arc C }   Page 60.

3. Left club Y Y Y arc C } (F) 2.
   Right " arc D arc C arc D arc C } 6. Page 63.
4. Left club Z Z Z arc D } (F) 2.
   Right " arc C arc D arc C arc D } 6. " 64.
5. Y arc Y D arc D (F) 3. Page 70.
6. D arc D Y arc Y (S) 3. " 71.
7. Left club Y Y C arc C } (T) 2.
   Right " D arc D Z Z } 6. Page 89.
8. Left club Z Z D arc D } (T) 3. " 90.
   Right " C arc C Y Y }
9. Y Y C arc C W W B arc B (F) 2. 6. Page 91.
10. Z Z D arc D X X A arc A (F) 2. 1. " 91.

TENTH LIST.

1. A W (F) 1. Page 47.
2. A W p (F) 1. " 85.
3. A W Z (F) 1. " 80.
4. A W p Z (F) 1. " 88.
5. A W (S) 1. " 47.
6. A W p (S) 1. " 85.
7. A W Z (S) 1. " 81.
8. A W p Z (S) 1. " 88.
9. B X Y (F) 1. " 81.
10. B X Y (S) 1. " 82.

ELEVENTH LIST.

1. n l Y C (F) 3. 2. Page 86.
2. Y D } (T) 2. Concert. " 78.
   Z C }
3. p A arc B W (F) 1. " 88.
4. W p p arc C (F) 6. " 91.
5. m Y l arc C (F) 6. " 92.
6. l arc D m Z (F) 6. " 92.
7. Left club Y C Y Y } (T) 2. " 77.
   Right " Z Z D Z }
8. Z D W (F) 2. " 82.
9. Z D W (S) 2. " 82.
10. Left club arc D arc Y } (F) 6. " 73.
    Right " arc Z arc C }
9*

☞ "Few are aware, until too late, of the importance of a healthy and vigorous bodily constitution. Such a constitution can only be secured by EXERCISE, temperance, and care in YOUTH." ◢

WAYLAND.

The revered late President of Brown University, whose wise and weighty words are here quoted, was himself an earnest advocate and constant exemplar of systematic physical culture. His sound judgment may be presumed to have been in full accord with that of many other eminent savans in awarding preëminence to the noble Fine Art illustrated in these pages. The Amateur closes his book, with a cordial invitation to every young man to give its contents a practical examination, being fully confident that every one who submits it to that test will frankly admit, that among the various modes of physical recreation now in vogue, no other one is so cheap, so convenient, so easily acquired, so free from liability to strain or accident, and at the same time so prompt and salutary in its effects on the muscular, respiratory and mental organization of its devotees as the interesting and manly exercise of

INDIAN CLUB SWINGING.

APPENDIX.

The following extracts contain the deliberate and recorded opinions of professional instructors and athletes, who, both from their thorough knowledge and long practice of the art of Indian club swinging are well qualified to speak of its merits and results :

1.

"This is a very graceful and beneficial exercise. It is easily acquired, and can be practiced at the office or dwelling of every person. There is nothing in the whole round of gymnastic performances that will be found of more essential service than this exercise with the clubs."

WM. WOOD.

2.

"For simplicity and convenience, they are unsurpassed by any other kind of apparatus, and half the fixtures of an ordinary gymnasium will not produce such a general development of the muscles, as a pair of clubs."

S. D. KEHOE.

3.

"As a means of imparting strength to the muscles of the arms, wrists and hands, in fact to the whole muscular system, I do not know of their equal."

J. C. HEENAN.

4.

"If their use is persevered in they will render the person who practices with them fully able to use his left arm almost as well as his right in hurling, flinging stones, lifting weights and simi-lar operations."

F. TOUCEY.

5.

"In the entire round of gymnastic exercises, no such efficient instruments as these have been discovered for bringing into ac-tion the muscles and tendons of the arms and trunk, which are generally less used than those of the legs."

PROF. HARRISON.

6.

"For indoor exercise there is nothing that can compete with them, the exercise far excelling the tedious motions required in using dumb-bells, pulley weights, &c., they being the same thing over and over again; while with clubs, new motions, changes and combinations are continually entering the mind, making it a source of pleasure, as well as benefiting the system."

S. T. WHEELWRIGHT.

7.

"All work done above the head, such as *swinging clubs*, or an axe or sledge, does excellent service in bringing to the abdominal muscles the length and elasticity they ought to have, and so con-tributing materially to the erect carriage of the body."

WM. BLAIKIE.

8.

"Although but two-thirds of the body, viz., from the loins upward, are called into operation in this exercise, its importance must be estimated by the fact that they are precisely those requir-ing constant artificial practice, being naturally most exempted from exertion."

EDWARD JAMES.

9.

"As a means of physical culture, the Indian Clubs stand pre-eminent among the varied apparatus of gymnastics now in use. The evolutions which the clubs are made to perform, in the hands of one accustomed to their use, are exceedingly graceful. Besides the great recommendation of simplicity, the Indian Club practice possesses the essential property of expanding the chest and exercising every muscle in the body concurrently. Note in the crowded thoroughfare of Broadway now and then an occasional passer-by, with well-knit and shapely form, firm and elastic step, broad-chested and full blooded, and you may mark him down as an expert with the clubs."

GUS HILL.

10.

"It demands but little muscular exertion, and such as it does require calls chiefly upon that portion of the system which it finds in a state of comparative repose."

PROF. WALKER.

11.

"For keeping the body in a healthy and vigorous condition there has yet been nothing invented, which for its simplicity and gracefulness can be favorably compared with the Indian Club exercise. Where the general building up of the muscles and sinews of the entire body is requisite, the medical profession unite with me in recommending club exercise, as they bring all parts of the body into play proportionately. My experience of many years, which has brought me in contact with the most prominent gymnasts and athletes of the country, warrants me to distinctly state, that there is no exercise so desirable or so attractive to the debilitated, or so positive in its results as the handling of Indian Clubs. Particularly is this the case for those who are wanting in vitality, and whose constitutions are impaired by the sluggish circulation of the blood. I may conscientiously say, a few moments' exercise with a light pair of clubs will accomplish more than all the medicines and tonics in the world."

M. BORNSTEIN.

CONTENTS.

INTRODUCTION.

SECTION 1.

SWINGS CONTAINING TWO CIRCLES.

* " Chief of chiefs, his regal word
All the river Sachems heard,
At his call the war-dance stirred,
Or was still once more."

SECTION 2.

SWINGS CONTAINING A CIRCLE AND AN ARC, OR TWO ARCS.

CHAPTER III.

TRIPLE AND QUADRUPLE MOVEMENTS.

SECTION 1.

SWINGS CONTAINING THREE OR MORE CIRCLES.

10

SECTION 2.

SWINGS CONTAINING THREE OR MORE MOVEMENTS, EITHER ARCS OR CIRCLES.

CHAPTER IV.

APPENDIX.